i so
don't do
famous

You so don't want to miss any of
Barrie Summy's books!

i so
don't do
mysteries

i so
don't do
spooky

i so
don't do
makeup

i so
don't do
famous

i so
don't do
famous

Barrie Summy

Delacorte Press

Text copyright © 2011 by Barbara Summy
Jacket photograph copyright © 2011 by Terry Vine

All rights reserved. Published in the United States by Delacorte Press, an imprint of Random House Children's Books, a division of Random House, Inc., New York.

Delacorte Press is a registered trademark and the colophon is a trademark of Random House, Inc.

Visit us on the Web! www.randomhouse.com
Educators and librarians, for a variety of teaching tools, visit us at www.randomhouse.com/teachers

Library of Congress Cataloging-in-Publication Data
Summy, Barrie.
I so don't do famous / by Barrie Summy. — 1st ed.
p. cm.
Summary: When thirteen-year-old Sherry Baldwin's essay wins a magazine contest, she, her father, and best friend Junie go to Hollywood, where she helps her ghost-detective mother and another ghost investigate a series of burglaries.
ISBN 978-0-385-73790-6 (hc)
ISBN 978-0-375-89947-8 (ebook)
[1. Ghosts—Fiction. 2. Mothers and daughters—Fiction. 3. Fathers and daughters—Fiction. 4. Celebrities—Fiction. 5. Burglary—Fiction. 6. Mystery and detective stories.] I. Title. II. Title: I so do not do famous.
PZ7.S9546Iaf 2011
[Fic]—dc22
2010023545

The text of this book is set in 12-point Century Schoolbook.
Book design by Marci Senders

Printed in the United States of America
10 9 8 7 6 5 4 3 2 1
First Edition

For the late Florence Moyer,
whose inspiration lives on

acknowledgments

Über thank-yous . . .

to the very talented (and also fun!) Wendy Loggia; the remarkable Rachel Vater; the hardworking team at Delacorte Press, including Beverly Horowitz, Marci Senders, Krista Vitola and Heather Lockwood Hughes.

to Kelly Hayes and Kathy Krevat for all their input and for believing in Sherry—although I know there were days they got sick of her!

to my cyber and sometimes real-life friends Misty Simon, Maureen McGowan, Alli Sinclair, Danita Cahill and Kathy Holmes. Will we ever be all together in the same room?

to Detective Sergeant Joe Bulkowski for his expert knowledge of all things police and for being so generous with said knowledge, even when texted late at night. Any errors are mine. An additional thank-you for the great fingerprinting presentation!

to Susan Patron, an authority on Hollywood and a very nice person. Once again, any errors are mine.

to Tatiana Garcia, who let me use her magnificent name for the Hollywood Police Department detective in this story. In real life, Tatiana loves Reese's Peanut Butter Cups, has a ponytail and is smart enough to solve the mystery by chapter five. Any negative characteristics associated with Detective Garcia are figments of my imagination.

to all my friends and family who allowed me to borrow and, in many cases, mix and match their names. A shout-out to Cameron Williams for being such a good sport and a great suspect.

finally, to Mark, Stan, Stephen, Drew and Claire. I love you guys.

chapter
one

Girlfriends. The mall. Clothes shopping.

Life doesn't get much better.

The food court is noisy and echoey. A ribbon of sun streams in from the skylight and bounces off the plastic lid of my soda. My elbow brushes against the mountain of shopping bags piled on the plastic seat next to me.

"Who has money left?" Brianna swishes a fry through a puddle of ketchup.

Junie wrinkles her nose to push up her glasses. "Probably only Sherry. She's the best shopper."

"Like twenty dollars," I say. I'm an expert bargain hunter. I have to be, given that I probably get the measliest allowance of any thirteen-year-old in

Phoenix. "But I'm really tempted to go back to Trendy's for that red swimsuit cover-up. It's only the end of July, and I could definitely use it around the pool."

"I wish I could wear red." Junie sighs. "But with this hair"—she hooks a few carroty strands behind her ear—"and these freckles"—she points to her face—"my color options are severely limited."

Junie's always been fixated on math and science and earning large quantities of As. She even got the award for the highest GPA last month at our seventh-grade end-of-the-year assembly. Recently, though, she branched out to my world of makeup, clothes and guys. Yay!

"At least you're not stuck with an oblong-shaped face. The next thing I spend money on is a haircut. Up to here." Brianna holds her hands flat at the level of her chin. "Saguaro Middle School counts on the eighth-grade girls to set the standard for fashion and beauty. No way I'm showing up looking like a horse."

"I'm growing my hair out," Junie says. "I'm totally broke."

"Too bad you two don't have a regular summer babysitting job like me." Brianna tilts the fries container in my direction. "I always have money coming in."

I grab a fry and peek at Junie, whose lips turn up

in the teeniest smile. Because we've been best friends since beginner swimming lessons years ago, we can pretty much read each other's minds. Yes, we're polar opposites in that she's all studious and grade-oriented, while I'm a social butterfly and middle-school fashionista. But I still know exactly what that little smile means: You may have money, Brianna Barnes, but we have love. And it's true. The bulk of the bags perched next to me are evidence of Brianna's steady income. But no height of shopping bags equals the amount of fun Junie and I are having chilling with Nick and Josh.

Josh Morton. Just thinking that name warms up my insides like a bowl of my stepmother's (aka The Ruler's) spicy lentil soup. Josh and I have been together for a little over four glorious months. He's a water polo player with the cutest chlorine-bleached hair and Lake Havasu blue eyes. He's crazy for music and video games and me. Josh goes to McDowell High School in the fall, which makes me frown because we won't be passing each other on campus anymore. Still, I'll be dating a high school guy!

Junie and Nick are newer to the couples scene. I've always had a bit of a problem with Nick and his nerdiness and sarcasm, but we're getting along better now.

My cell phone rings. A number I don't recognize is on the screen. My index finger hovers over the keypad. My dad and The Ruler limit my phone minutes, and they're super strict about it.

Brianna rolls her eyes. "Just answer it."

"Hello," I say.

"Hi," says a female voice. "I'm looking for Sherlock Holmes Baldwin."

"Speaking."

"This is Dear Elle from *Hollywood Girl* magazine."

My heart stops. Dear Elle? The love advice columnist who knows anything and everything about relationships? From the magazine I read without fail every month?

"Hello? Are you there?" Dear Elle asks.

My heart is still in jammed mode, but my vocal cords kick into gear. "I am," I say in a raspy, nervous voice.

"Well, Sherlock, I'm calling to say congratulations! Your essay on true love won first place in the *Hollywood Girl* contest."

Emotion bubbles from the tips of my fuchsia-painted toenails through my legs, swirls around my stomach and my chest, then rushes up my throat to my mouth, where it bursts forth in a big scream.

Both Junie and Brianna jump up from their side of the table and dash to me. "What is it? What's going on?"

My hands flutter and flap in the air. "I won. I won. I won."

"That's right," Dear Elle says. "You won a week in

Hollywood for you, your legal guardian and a friend. All paid for by the magazine. Also, there will be a special dinner at the Roosevelt Hotel, honoring you and various magazine employees."

"I won. I won. I won." I can't seem to turn myself off.

"I'll need to go over the details with your legal guardian," Dear Elle says.

I take a deep breath and manage to give her my home phone number. Before disconnecting, Dear Elle compliments me on my essay and my understanding of true love. She explains that the essay and my photo will be in the next issue and posted even sooner on the magazine's website.

"I'm looking forward to meeting you!" she says, clicking off.

Wow.

Wow!

"My essay on true love won first place in the *Hollywood Girl* contest!" I blurt out to my friends.

Brianna squeals.

"Awesome!" Junie says.

"I can't believe I was just talking to Dear Elle. I just can't believe it." My hands are a flapping blur.

The people at the table next to us pick up their trays and move.

"So, you're like a love expert?" Brianna says. "Tell me something from your essay."

"Like what? It's five hundred words long." I chew

on my lip. "How about this?" I clear my throat. " 'Love shows up when you least expect it. Like a pop quiz.' "

"Ooooh, that's heavy," Brianna says.

"Thank you." My hands settle on the table.

"Too bad you didn't think to ask Dear Elle about your relationship with Josh," Brianna says. "Perfect opportunity. You wouldn't have to wait for the answer to be published."

"What?" I stare at her. Brianna has a way of tossing stuff into a conversation like she's throwing a ball through a window. "Why would I have questions about Josh?"

She shrugs.

"I vaguely remember reading about the contest when I borrowed a stack of your magazines." Junie sips her drink. "What's the prize again?"

"A trip to Hollywood for a week! For me, a parent and a friend! And I get to go to an awards dinner with Dear Elle!"

"A trip to Hollywood!" Junie's eyes flash with excitement.

"I wonder what diamond she'll wear at the dinner." Brianna pops another fry in her mouth.

"I wish I'd asked her that," I say. Dear Elle always wears a diamond when she's out in public because a diamond is the universal symbol for true love, and she's the ambassador.

"Who'll take you?" Junie asks. "The Ruler or your dad?"

"The Ruler, I'm assuming. In a million years, I can't see my dad missing work for Hollywood and an award about true love."

"Too bad you can't take two friends." Brianna stares down at her nails, picking at the polish. "Anyway, I committed to this dumb babysitting job, and it goes the whole way to the end of August."

"For me"—Junie's face is flushed—"the Hollywood trip is perfect timing. Stars! Fame! Fortune!" She holds her hands up, framing each word.

I nod, waiting for her to make sense.

"Exactly what the students want to read," Junie says. "Exactly."

"What students?" Brianna and I ask together.

"At school." Junie picks up her deep-fried cheese on a stick. "Where I'm the new editor of the online paper." She waves the cheese. "I'll kick off the school year with stories and photos from our trip to Hollywood. I'll research L.A., Hollywood, Beverly Hills, celebrities, tourist attractions, trivia! I'll know everything there is to know before we leave! This will be the strongest September our paper has ever seen!"

I've never heard Junie talk so fast. Or with so many exclamation points.

I watch while she nibbles along the edge of her cheese. I am not feeling good about what I'm going to say next. I'm feeling a little guilty. Maybe even a lot guilty. But Junie is a good friend. Surely she'll understand where I'm coming from. If not today, then tomorrow.

"Junie"—I reach across the table and place a hand on her shoulder—"the essay is actually about true love. Not true friendship." I take a deep breath. "When you look at it that way, don't you think this would be the coolest, most romantic trip to take with Josh?"

chapter
two

Up in my bedroom, I flip open the lid of my aquarium and sprinkle in fish food. My two beautiful bala sharks, Cindy and Prince, zip to the flakes. Their scales glitter and gleam. They're happy and well fed and in love. Sometimes I envy their simple life.

My chest feels tight, like a huge rock is squishing it. At the mall, when I said I was taking Josh to Hollywood, Junie's face turned white and splotchy. Even Brianna lost her chattiness.

I called Josh while I was walking home, but he didn't pick up. I didn't leave a message, because I want to hear his reaction to the big news. I'm guessing polo practice ran over. Josh is already working out with the high school team. He doesn't miss a chance to stay late to help clean up the deck. He's trying hard to make a good impression on the coach.

I flop down on my bed. Lying on my stomach, my chin resting on crossed elbows, I text him.

No reply.

I stare at the fish. "Maybe Josh's phone is charging," I say to Cindy as she whisks by. "He's bad about letting the battery run down." Her scales gleam and glisten. "What should I do?"

With a flick of her almost translucent tail, she chases Prince through the little castle at the bottom of the tank. I can tell she's thinking what I'm thinking.

Call his house phone.

"Hello?" Vicki, Josh's mom, answers. She's a hairdresser with hip highlights, the best nails and a talent for walking in three-inch-high heels. She's super friendly and gabby.

"Hi, it's me. Sherry, that is." And then my words trip all over themselves in a hurry to let the world know about my amazing prize. "I just won a trip to Hollywood! By entering an essay I wrote!"

"Cool beans!" Vicki says. "Does Josh know?"

"Not yet."

"Let me give you to him. He's right next to me. That is so exciting, Sherry." Her voice fades a little, but I can still hear her clearly. "Josh, stop playing games on your phone. It's Sherry with great news."

"Yeah?" he says.

In that one word, I can tell Josh isn't in a great mood. I'm very in tune with people and their emotions. This is probably what helped me write an intelligent, intuitive essay on love. Lucky for Josh, I have the news that will completely change his mood.

"Are you sitting down?" I ask. "You will not believe this."

"What?" Josh says.

"So, I wrote an essay on true love for a magazine contest. A couple of months ago. I never for a second thought I'd win. I mean, think how many people enter. But I totally did. I came in first!"

"Wow," Josh says. "Congrats."

"Guess what the prize is?" But I'm too excited to wait for his guess and barrel on. "You. Me. Hollywood. Palm trees. The Walk of Fame. The wax museum." I pause for a breath. "Well, all that and The Ruler, too."

"Uh, when?"

"We need to leave in about a week. To be there for the awards dinner," I say. "We are going to have the most fabulous time!"

"I don't know, Sherry—"

I stop him right there because I have a bad feeling, like too much of The Ruler's heavy, bricklike wheat bread is digesting in my stomach. I don't want Josh to say anything about how it might be impossibly tough to talk our parents into the trip. No. That kind of negative thinking is better left in your head and not given a voice in the outside world.

"Josh," I say, "let's meet at Jazzed-Up Juice and come up with a strategy for getting our parents on board. My treat."

Good thing I hung on to that twenty dollars.

I brush my hair, reapply lip gloss and walk back to the mall. Over the years, it's like I've worn my own personal path from our front door to the entrance of the Phoenix Mall.

Once inside the big glass doors, I head to Jazzed-Up Juice. It's a smallish restaurant close to Video World and across from the food court. Pretty popular with the middle-school crowd, it's sort of our date place. Josh and I have shared gallons of smoothies here. We even have our table, in the back corner.

Josh beat me, probably because he skateboarded over. He's already seated, drumming his fingers on the tabletop, staring off into space.

Just watching him, my heart expands until it's bumping against my rib cage.

He looks up. His azure Camel's Breath band T-shirt picks up the blue in his eyes. He sees me. And offers up a wan smile. Yikes. He really is in a crummy mood. I wonder if something went down at polo. Well, one thing's for sure. He'll be feeling way better in a few minutes. Most problems in life can be fixed with a smoothie, my sense of humor and a trip to California.

I smile big and point to the menu.

He nods, and a lock of his shaggy hair falls across one eyebrow.

Once I've got a large Orange-Banana Workout and two bendy straws, I pick my way through the tables and chairs and plunk down across from Josh. I poke the straws into the thick liquid, and we both take a long slurp.

Leaning back, I stretch out my legs. "Tough day?"

"Not particularly." Josh crosses his arms.

"A trip to Hollywood. Isn't it just too incredible?" I say, trying to cheer him up. "I'm gonna start talking to The Ruler tonight about you. Sort of work her up to it." I take a long drink. "What about your parents? Will they be cool with it?"

"With what?"

I lean forward and place my hands on either side of his face. "Earth to Josh. Earth to Josh."

"I'm listening."

I drop my hands. "Will your parents be cool about you coming to Hollywood with The Ruler and me?"

"I don't know. . . ." Josh looks down.

"Let's do this. I'll talk The Ruler into it first." I sip. "Then we'll have her call your mom."

"No, I meant I don't know that I want to go." Josh

pulls his phone from his shorts pocket and starts spinning it on the table.

"What? Josh! We're talking Hollywood, California," I screech. "How could you possibly pass up a super fun opportunity like that?"

"Polo." Josh watches his phone turning and glinting. "I might get to be on taxi squad. And practice with the varsity team. As a freshman."

Taxi schmaxi. "We're talking *one* week of summer vacation." I cross my arms. "Hollywood always trumps polo."

Josh looks up at me. "Not in my world."

chapter
three

My last view of Josh is him striding out of Jazzed-Up Juice, hitching up his sagging jeans, which drop right back down to his hips.

I sit quietly, swirling my straw around in the smoothie. It bumps into Josh's straw, which I pull out and drop on the table. A splash of pink lands on the front of my T-shirt.

I can think of a million things I should've said. Like I'm actually more important than water polo. And do you even want to read my winning essay? People would give their right arm to win an all-expenses-paid trip to Hollywood!

Tears pool in my eyes, and a golf ball–sized lump

lodges in my throat. How did something so right turn so very wrong? Guys!

I toss the rest of the smoothie and head to the Naked Makeup kiosk where Junie's seventeen-year-old cousin, Amber, works part-time. Amber is the only real-life boy expert I know. She's not always nice to me or Junie, but I'm hoping she'll help me make sense of today's strangeness with Josh.

From a couple of stores away, I can see Amber perched on a stool by the cash register, filing her nails. Her well-behaved shoulder-length straight blond hair swings slightly with her hand movements. She looks like a poster for Best-Put-Together Teen.

I'm practically standing on the toes of Amber's cute slingbacks before she notices me. She stops filing. Her emery board hovers above a nail. "You here to buy product, Sherry?"

"Actually, I need advice," I say, making sure I sound humble.

Amber returns to filing. Her right ring finger, to be exact. "Uh-huh."

"I can't figure Josh out." I tell her about winning the contest and Josh not answering his cell and then refusing to go to Hollywood.

The emery board falls to the counter. "You won the true-love essay contest? And I didn't even help you." She high-fives me. "Way to go!"

"Thanks," I say, a flame of pride flickering in my chest.

"Dear Elle is like a goddess," Amber says. And she starts reminiscing about all the Dear Elle columns she read and how they related to this or that boyfriend.

"Now, about Josh." She picks up the emery board. "Is he your only boyfriend?"

"What?" I sputter. "Yes!"

"That is so your issue." The emery board weaves across the tip of her nail. "You need a BUB."

"A BUB?"

"A Back-Up Boyfriend." Amber blows nail dust in the air. "Then when your boyfriend isn't behaving himself, you have your BUB waiting for your call."

Two boyfriends? That sounds worse than two tests in the same day. "I don't think that's the answer for me."

Amber shoots me a look like I'm a dog who won't learn to heel. "Fine. If you're sticking to one, then trade up to a WAB."

"A WAB?"

"A boyfriend with Wheels and Bank."

"Bank?" I feel like I'm trapped in a weird Monopoly game of romance.

"As in 'earns money.'" Amber nods, and the fluorescent lighting glints off her hair like she's wearing

17

a crown. "Can you think of a guy with a driver's license and a part-time job?"

"Amber, I'm thirteen. My dad and The Ruler will never let me go out with a guy old enough to drive and work."

"Well"—she shrugs her slender shoulders—"then you're stuck fishing in the middle-school, high-school boy pool." With her pinkie, Amber pulls open a small drawer next to the register. She drops in the emery board and picks up a tiny jar. "Where you'll only catch the dregs."

"The DREGS?" I say. "What's that code for?"

Amber rolls her kohl-outlined eyes. "It's not code for anything. Guys who are the dregs are gross and lame. Like the leftover gunk at the bottom of a coffeepot."

I make an O with my thumb and index finger. "Gotcha." It's a mystery how I won the true-love essay contest with such gaping holes in my dating knowledge.

"Still"—Amber unscrews the jar lid and scoops out a smidgen of pale cream—"there's gotta be a BUB, even a sad WAB, swimming around in your pool."

"But I don't want a BUB or a WAB, and definitely not the dregs," I wail. "I just want Josh to go to Hollywood with me."

Amber frowns at me. "Knock it off, Sherry. You never know when a customer's going to show up."

"Okay, okay." I gulp a couple of times, getting my-self under control. "Look, Amber, Josh is starting high school in a few weeks. Maybe that's the prob-lem. I look like an eighth-grade baby."

She briefly closes her lavender-colored eyelids and waves her hand in the air, dismissing my concerns. "Don't be ridiculous. I always date up. Always. I can't even remember the last time I went out with someone my own age. Everyone should date up."

"Everyone can't date up. Look at the guys you're dating. They're dating down."

"No, Sherry, they're dating *me*." With small circu-lar movements, Amber rubs the cream into her cuti-cles, releasing a fresh peppermint smell into the air. "Here's my final advice. Dump Josh before he dumps you. Then go to Hollywood and have the time of your life."

She sashays to the end of the kiosk, where an older woman with bluish hair approaches the rack of mas-caras. "Norma," she sings out, "we just got a ship-ment of moisturizing eye shadows. I was hoping you'd stop by."

Dazed, I plod to the exit, forcing one foot in front of the other, sticking to the lines in the linoleum floor so that I don't wander off track.

The whole way there, Amber's woeful words ping-pong around my brain. "You need a BUB." "Trade up to a WAB." "Dump Josh before he dumps you." I hit

19

my palm against the side of my head, trying to shake her words loose and out into the mall. But they won't leave. Because Amber knows boys. And I only know Josh.

On autopilot, I walk home, thinking, thinking, thinking. The house is silent. I'm the only one there. I climb up to my room and sit cross-legged on my bed. I retrieve my cell from my purse and press number two, speed dial for Josh.

"Hey," he says in a monotone voice.

"So, what's really going on?" I ask, then hold my breath.

"I don't know, Sherry." He pauses. "I mean, I'm gonna be in high school this fall."

"Uh-huh." A little air escapes through my mouth.

"And I'll be busy with high school stuff. And polo and swim."

"Uh-huh." A little more air puffs out. But for the most part, I'm still as a stone. It's like if I don't move, I can't feel the pain.

"I think, uh, maybe we need a, uh, break from each other," Josh says in a low voice.

"Okay," I say. "Okay."

I hit End and slump over like a snail, my head resting on my arms, my eyes closed. I stay in this sad position for what feels like forever but is probably less.

In the distance, the doorbell rings. The Ruler's

voice is muted and mumbling. I don't even know when she came home.

The flap-flap of approaching flip-flops gets louder. Junie and Brianna. We planned to do our nails this evening. Before I turned into a blob of depression.

"Sherry," Junie says softly, coming into my room. "Are you okay?"

"Are you sick?" Brianna shakes my shoulder. "Are you unconscious?"

I lift my heavy head and turn toward the wall.

"Can unconscious people do that?" Brianna asks Junie.

"She's not unconscious," Junie says. She rubs my back. "What's wrong?"

Tears squeeze through my closed lids. I might actually go unconscious. There's a lump in my throat that's so huge it's probably restricting airflow to my brain. "Josh," I manage to squeeze out.

"Josh is unconscious?" Brianna asks.

"No," I say hoarsely.

"What could be so wrong with Josh," Brianna says, "that Sherry can't even talk about it?"

"Brianna. Stop." Junie's voice is sharp with annoyance. She's so smart. She always unscrambles a situation faster than Brianna. Often faster than me. She can tell I'm a wreck. "Be useful. Get some water."

Brianna trundles off to the bathroom I share with my brother, Sam.

"Josh and I broke up," I whisper.

Junie hugs me. "I'm sorry."

Brianna returns with a cup of water and holds it out to me. I pull myself to a sitting position and drink.

"What's going on?" Brianna says. "What'd I miss?"

"Brianna!" Junie says. "Have some tact."

"It's okay." I hold the cool cup against my forehead. "She's gonna find out at some point. Everyone is."

"What? What?" Brianna's head whips at windmill speed from me to Junie, then back to me.

"Josh and I broke up." It's easier to say the second time.

Brianna gasps and her mouth gapes. She slaps a hand over it, and stares at me with big round eyes. She lowers her hand. "That's so sad. And right after you wrote an essay on true love. Just pitiful." She pauses. "You'll have a lot of free time now. Want me to help you find a full-time babysitting job? I bet we could get you working by next week at the latest."

"No," Junie says, "she's going to Hollywood."

"You're still going?" Brianna asks, her eyes all wide again. "Without Josh?"

"Of course, she is," Junie says. "It's a breakup. She's not dead."

The thought of Hollywood makes my heart beat a little faster. Yes, it *is* broken and jagged and jabbing into me. But Junie's right. I'm alive.

I set the cup on my nightstand. "Brianna, some things are bigger than a broken heart. And Hollywood is one of those things."

"I'm starting to understand why your essay won," Brianna says. "You're wise beyond your years, Sherry. Übermature."

"So, Junie," I say, "up for a trip?"

Junie beams. "Definitely." And she's such a bona fide best friend that she doesn't say another word.

chapter
four

Our house has the perfect place for eavesdropping—the landing at the top of the stairs. I'm crouched there now in the dark.

While The Ruler and my dad were loading the dishwasher I overheard her say quietly, "We need to talk about Sherry."

Say what? At dinner, everyone was thrilled over my win and sad about my breakup. What could The Ruler and my dad possibly have to talk about concerning me?

Sam's been in bed for a while. Supposedly, I'm safely tucked away in my room, reading *Rebecca,* my summer English assignment. Every few days, I pull the book out of my desk drawer and dog-ear a couple of pages. I'll check out SparkNotes right before school starts.

Below me and down the hall, the kitchen light switches off. The fluorescent hall light flickers on and warms up to a dull, environmentally friendly blue. Dad and Paula are moving to the living room, their chatting ground.

I shift slightly, fading into the shadowy stripe of the banister. I peer through the rails.

The Ruler leads the way, taking small steps in her Naturalizer slippers while balancing a mug of calming chamomile tea. My dad pads along behind her in bare feet, a can of diet soda in his hand. He stops and sips, then sighs. He's probably imagining a bowl mounded high with French vanilla ice cream.

The couch cushions breathe out as my dad and The Ruler settle in. Their heads bobble like they have spring necks.

Dad stretches out an arm with the remote, and Céline Dion's vocals soar through the living room. My dad has a love affair going with that singer. If she ever knocked at our front door, he'd follow her through the streets of Phoenix like she was the Pied Piper.

"What's going on with Sherry?" My dad spaces each word apart, like he's expecting bad news.

The Ruler says something.

I cup my ear.

My dad responds. Something.

Ack. I cannot hear. Like a cat sneaking up on a mouse, I slowly scoot down a couple of steps. I press my cheek against the cool metal railing, my ear jutting through the bars. What are these people saying about me?

"You really think I should go?" Dad crosses, then uncrosses his feet at the ankles, then finally rests them side by side on the coffee table.

"It'd be great bonding time for you two. Also, I can't miss the robotics meeting," The Ruler says. "And it'd be really good for Sherry to leave town, attend the awards ceremony and get some distance between her and this breakup."

The Ruler's sending Dad to Hollywood with Junie and me?

"I have a few clients in Los Angeles I could see while I'm out there," my dad says.

"Sure." The Ruler bends forward to gather up her knitting. "The magazine pays for the tickets, but you need to talk with Sherry about exact dates. And to let her know you're going, of course."

My dad's feet hit the floor.

"I'm sure she's already asleep, Bob. She always dozes off reading *Rebecca*." The Ruler's needles click rhythmically. "Talk to her tomorrow, then we'll touch base with Junie's parents."

I crab-walk backward. Across the carpeted landing, into my bedroom, grazing my shoulder on the door-jamb.

There's someone else I need to invite on the trip. My mom.

My mom was a cop with the Phoenix Police Department. She died in the line of duty a couple of years ago. After her death, she enrolled in the Academy of Spirits, an organization that trains ghosts to protect humans. At first, she was totally flunking her classes. To boost her dismal grades, she recruited me as her partner in mystery solving. Now she's acing school and was recently loaned out to a foreign Academy for a few months.

I wait until my house is the kind of calm and quiet you get when everyone's in bed. Then I scrounge in my desk drawer for a Ziploc bag of coffee beans, toss on a sweatshirt and tiptoe downstairs and through the kitchen. A bright moon lights up our backyard. I tramp across the lawn to the ornamental pear tree in the corner of the yard. My mom planted this tree when I was born, and it's where I have the best luck getting in touch with her.

I throw a leg over the lowest branch and hoist my-self up. Once I'm sitting, my back scrunched against the trunk, I open the Ziploc bag and let the smell of coffee waft through the night air. I close my eyes and think mom thoughts.

I wait.

The night is still. Crickets chirp. An owl hoots off in the distance.

I wait some more. Calling a ghost can take patience.

Lately, my mother and I have been in contact way less frequently because her work with the foreign Academy doesn't include me.

All of a sudden, the leaves shudder in a whoosh of java-scented air. Ghosts smell like something important from their mortal life. My mother was a coffee fanatic. The branch bobs as she settles next to me.

"Hi, Sherry," she says brightly. "How are you? I've missed you."

At the sound of her voice, a lump clogs my throat. "Josh and I broke up." My eyes spill over with tears.

"Oh, pumpkin, I'm so sorry." There's a feathery touch where she's smoothing my forehead.

I would give anything for a hug. Or even a few minutes of Real Time, where I can actually see her and be with her.

"When did it happen?" she asks gently.

I choke out the story. Then I add, "I'm not walking around like a zombie or whatever. I have chunks of time when I'm pretty much fine and not even thinking about the breakup. But then, sometimes I have pain with every heartbeat. With every breath. With every song on the radio. My emotions are totally whacked out."

"Sounds normal. The sadness comes and goes in waves," my mom says. "But I'm sorry you're having to go through it."

Caw. Caw. A cactus wren flaps in and wraps his yellow feet around the branch directly above us. The cactus wren—our state bird and my grandfather. Grandpa died of a heart attack a few years ago. He opted to take on the shape of a wren and the position of mascot for the Academy of Spirits. He's tough to understand, but has a solid sense of direction and really comes through when we're hot on the trail of a clue.

"Hi, Grandpa." I wipe my eyes with the back of my hand.

"Sherry and Josh broke up," my mom tells him.

He clucks sympathetically.

"How's Grandma?" I ask.

"Good," he croaks. "Still recovering."

"What's happened to Grandma?" my mom asks, concerned.

"Hip surgery," Grandpa says.

"Grandpa's hanging out with her a bunch," I say. "Still hoping she'll make the connection that he's no ordinary wren."

Grandpa shakes his little balding head to indicate

that no, Grandma hasn't figured out his true identity. My grandmother is all New Agey, with herbs and crystals and auras, but she can't see Grandpa for who he really is.

"I didn't realize she was having surgery." My mother sighs. "Some days life moves too quickly, and I feel that I'm missing out. Especially right now while I'm working for the foreign Academy." Our branch jiggles. I bet my mom is sitting in her favorite position, one leg crossed over the other, her foot swinging back and forth. "Sherry, can you stay busy? With Junie? And try to keep your mind off Josh? Wallowing is not healthy."

I smack my forehead. I think this breakup is affecting my memory. "I have huge news. Huge California news!" I spill.

"I am so proud of you!" my mom says, all enthusiastic.

Grandpa's beak opens, and out pours a long string of Russian-sounding syllables.

I shrug. From the way his dark birdy eyes are flashing, I'm sure he said something enthusiastic too.

"Grandpa believes that he and your grandmother helped you win because they're an excellent example of true love," Mom translates. "Obviously, true love is in your genes."

Nice to know, because at the moment it feels more like failed love is in my genes. I grimace inside.

30

Grandpa flutters above me. He briefly places a tattered wing across his tiny feathered chest. "Back to Grandma."

I wave as he becomes a dark speck against the white moon.

I turn to the space next to me. "Mom, guess where I'll be staying? Three clues." I extend a finger. "The year is 1929." I hold up a second finger. "The address is 7000 Hollywood Boulevard." I waggle a third finger. "The event is the Academy Awards."

"The Roosevelt Hotel!" My mother gasps. "What if your awards dinner is held in the Blossom Ballroom? My baby getting an award in the same room where the first Oscar was given out!" The branch shakes more. Her leg must be bouncing a mile a minute. "I *have* to be there."

"I want you to be there." And now that I've said it aloud, I realize just how much I do want my mom to come to Hollywood. Some of my best memories are of watching the Academy Awards together. The two of us on the couch with a giant bowl of buttered popcorn, the TV blaring, our guesses written down in sealed envelopes on the coffee table.

My hand clenches in excited anticipation.

"And Marilyn Monroe's ghost shows up in a mirror at the Roosevelt," she says. "You know how long I've been fascinated by the mystery surrounding her death."

My elbow bends.

"I'm sure the foreign Academy would love to tie up the loose ends on that case. Any academy would," Mom says. "What if I approached the administration about working the Marilyn Monroe mystery? It wouldn't exactly be a vacation for me, but I could attend your awards ceremony. We could hang out and do some touristy things together in Hollywood."

"Yes, yes, yes!" I punch the air with a victory fist.

chapter
five

Things I do to get ready for Hollywood:
• chores to earn extra spending money
• shop for travel-sized shampoo, conditioner, deodorant, toothpaste; magazines and snacks for plane ride; swimsuit cover-up from Trendy's
• convince Brianna that we will not be constantly texting her our every move because we don't have unlimited texting
• give my brother explicit instructions on how to look after my fish
• visit my grandmother
Things I don't do:
• text Josh
• phone Josh

- see Josh
- stop thinking about Josh

Finally, it arrives—the day of our trip.

The plane ride from Phoenix to LAX—Los Angeles International Airport—is short. Junie and I talk for the entire flight. My dad starts off reading a business book, but we're barely in the air before his head is bobbing and his book tumbles to the pull-out tray table.

The plane lands and we follow signs to the baggage area. While we're waiting for the carousel to crank up, my dad pulls a packet of papers from the front of his carry-on. He slaps at his jeans pockets, trying to locate his reading glasses. "Let's look at the information Paula typed up."

"Dad, seriously." I watch for my bag as the carousel jerks to life. "Junie and I memorized the itinerary."

"Next is a limo ride to the hotel," Junie says.

We pull off our luggage, then head for the exit. Junie strides fast, which she can do easily, as her suitcase is the size of a tissue box. I'm a little worried that she didn't pack enough clothes.

We drag our bags through the automatic doors. It's warm. It's muggy. It's noisy with honking horns and screeching cars.

A hand on her forehead to shade her eyes, Junie

scans the horizon. I dig through my purse for my new blingy sunglasses. My dad catches his breath.

"Here it comes," Junie sings out.

Shining and gleaming in the California sun, a sleek black stretch limo glides up beside us.

I run my palm along the fender. I thought I'd have to wait until my prom to snag a ride in a limo.

Junie knocks on the front passenger's window.

The driver's door yawns open, and a guy clambers out. A guy Amber would totally glom onto. He's twentyish, with bleached-blond hair, a beach tan and mirrored sunglasses. He's wearing a white T-shirt, cutoffs and flip-flops. This guy's a WAB and a BUB all rolled into a cute California package.

He holds up a piece of cardboard with one word on it: SHERRY. "This name apply to any of you?"

"Me." I give a half-wave.

"*Hollywood Girl* sent me to take you to the Roosevelt." He leans through the open door and presses a button to pop the trunk. "This your party?"

"Yeah. My dad and my friend Junie." I gesture with a shoulder.

Dad sticks out an arm.

"Hello, sir." The chauffeur shakes my dad's hand. "Welcome to the City of Angels. I'm Stephen." He grabs our bags and swings them into the back of the vehicle.

We hop in, scooting along the spotless white leather seats. Junie and I ooh and ahh over the adorable TV and the minibar.

We're barely buckled up when Stephen peels out into the airport traffic. Zooming away from a trail of horn blasts, we zip onto a freeway with about thirty different lanes, each one filled with vehicles speeding faster than their neighbors.

Hello, California!

And then we arrive at 7000 Hollywood Boulevard. The Roosevelt stands tall and white, with its name in block letters on the roof. We check in and ride the elevator up to the eighth floor and our adjoining rooms. Dad unlocks his door first. He drops into a corduroy chair like he's arriving home from a grueling day at the office. With a yawn the size of the Grand Canyon, he stretches his arms up above his head. "I need to phone Paula and then make some business calls to set up meetings for the next few days."

And take a nap with ESPN on in the background, I think.

"Do you girls want to watch cartoons or something in your room?"

"Cartoons? Uh, Dad, we're *middle* schoolers, not *pre*schoolers?" And we're on vacation in a hotel with a few resident ghosts and a load of movie-star history.

A hotel that's located right in the thick of things on Hollywood Boulevard. There will be no cartoons in our immediate future.

"Actually, Junie and I want to scope out where the awards ceremony will be, find the pool and restaurants, and see if there's a gift shop."

"Got it." He yawns again. "Don't leave the hotel grounds and stay in touch." He picks up the remote.

Junie and I take the elevator back to the lobby. By the check-in counter is a white sandwich board announcing today's various functions. We're at the top of the list:

6 p.m.: Blossom Ballroom
<u>Hollywood Girl</u> Dinner and Awards
(by invitation only)

Across from the counter, there are groupings of coffee tables and overstuffed leather couches and chairs. We plop down at the side of the room. I stretch out on a wide chaise longue, crossing my legs at the ankles. My pink toenails wink in the dim light.

Junie's beside me, also reclining on a chaise longue. She hauls her backpack up next to her hip, tugs open the zipper and pulls out a spreadsheet. "I want to narrow down places we can visit while we're here. Places I can write about, that is." She gnaws on the end of her pen. "Definitely the attractions within walking distance, like Grauman's Chinese Theatre, Madame Tussauds, the Walk of Fame and the Kodak Theatre."

"Those sound good," I say. "And how about shopping on Rodeo Drive? Also, my mom mentioned Pink's hot-dog stand. I'm salivating at the thought of a chili dog."

"It's so cool that your mom's coming out." Junie looks up from her list. "When will she arrive?"

I shrug. "In time for the awards dinner. That's all I know."

Junie jots away in her no-nonsense cursive. "I want to write about some off-the-beaten-track places too."

"Not too off-the-beaten-track, though, right?" Sometimes I worry about Junie and how she doesn't totally relate to the typical teen.

She taps the pen on her thigh. "Well, like the Petersen Automotive Museum and the Museum of Neon Art."

"You might want to rethink that plan." I hold my hand up like a stop sign. "I'm your target reader, and I have zero interest in reading about those places."

Junie juts out her chin. Just an inch or even less. But when you've been friends with someone for as long I've been friends with Junie, you can read all the body language. When Junie juts out her chin, she's moving into stubborn mode. And once she's in stubborn mode, there's no budging her.

Beep. She has a text.

My chest tightens. Because only a few people text Junie: me, Brianna and Nick. It's obviously not me. We're supposed to text Brianna first so she doesn't use up a bunch of our texts with boring stuff about her babysitting job. Which narrows it down to Nick. So, Junie's relatively new boyfriend, Nick, is texting her. Nick, who sometimes hangs out with Josh!

chapter
six

Junie reads her text message, smiles, then thumbs in a reply.

"Is it Nick?" My heart speeds up. "What'd he say? Is he with Josh? How's Josh?"

"He's not with Josh." Junie looks at the floor.

And that look speaks volumes. "But he *was* with Josh?"

"How do you do that?" Junie stares at me. "It's like you get inside my head."

"I don't know exactly. I think partly it's from hanging out with you for years and partly from learning to be an observant detective." I fish in my purse for gum, slide out a piece, then toss the package at Junie. "So, what were Josh and Nick up to?"

"Josh phoned Nick." She hands the gum back to me, without taking a piece.

"Because he's überdepressed about breaking up with me and needed a friend to talk to?" I clasp a hand to my heart. "I almost feel a little sorry for him. It's no fun going through a breakup."

Junie sits unmoving like the stone statue of the saguaro cactus in the courtyard at school.

"Oh, I get it." I unwrap the gum and pop it in my mouth. "He feels even worse now that we're out here in California on the trip he gave up."

Junie closes her eyes.

"What? What is it?"

"Josh called Nick because the high-school water polo coach needed someone to videotape a few scrimmages," she says softly.

I slump down in my chaise longue, deflated like a day-old balloon. Josh isn't überdepressed. He probably hasn't wasted one fraction of one second missing me. I'd slide farther down the chair, but that would land me on the tile floor.

"Josh hasn't figured out yet what he's lost." Beside me, Junie slumps in sympathy. "But he will, Sherry. I just know it."

We sit in silence. I'm letting the waves of sadness wash over me, remembering my mother's words about how this will pass and I'll feel okay again.

Trapped in my own little world, at first I don't

notice the two teen girls skipping around the lounge until one of them laughs loudly. They're checking out all the little sitting areas.

When they arrive at us, they stop. Both girls have chin-length brown hair, knit tank tops and short skirts. The kind of short skirt that's against our school's dress code. One of the girls has a ring through her nose and the cutest silver bracelet with a dog charm. The other has an eyebrow bar and lavender eye shadow. They're wearing flip-flops with HOLLYWOOD HIGH SCHOOL stamped across the strap.

They glance at Junie, smile vacantly, then turn to me.

Eyebrow Bar Girl says, "Sherlock Baldwin?"

"Uh, yes." I scoot to a sitting position. These people do not look even remotely familiar.

Nose Ring Girl squeals. "I can't believe it's actually you." She punches Eyebrow Bar Girl in the arm. "It's her. We found her. Yay us!"

Junie's forehead is creased with a thick line of confusion. These girls don't look familiar to her either.

"I'm sorry," I say. "Do I know you guys?"

Nose Ring Girl's eyes sparkle. "I'm Lorraine. I'm super happy to meet you."

"I'm Stef," Eyebrow Bar Girl says.

"How do you know Sherry?" Junie asks.

"Sherry? So cute!" Lorraine's eyes sparkle. "Does everyone call you Sherry? Not Sherlock?"

"I only get Sherlock during roll call on the first day of school," I say. "And when my parents are mad at me."

"Same for me with 'Stefanie.'" Stef nods.

"Why were you looking for Sherry?" Junie asks. She's more suspicious of people, where I'm more open and friendly.

"To say congratulations," Stef says.

"We love your essay about true love. Love it. Adore it. Dig it." Lorraine tugs on the hem of her skirt.

I don't mention there isn't enough material for that skirt to stay decent for any length of time. "Thank you." I feel kind of floaty and rock-starrish.

"I read the whole thing." Lorraine beams. "And that's saying a lot because I don't read. Except for Dear Elle's column."

"With your essay, it's like you're talking straight to my heart." Stef taps her chest. "Direct, honest, real. You so know your stuff."

"Wow. Thanks." I check my feet to make sure they're still firmly on the ground. "I had to rewrite it a couple of times."

"And your photo?" Lorraine sighs. "Adorable. Great makeup."

"Thank you," I say again. "I did it myself." Who knew I'd have fans!

43

"Sherry's essay wasn't on the *Hollywood Girl* website the last time I looked," Junie says. "I wonder when they went live with it."

"Don't have a clue." Lorraine glances at Junie. "Sometime before lunch today. Because that's when we read it."

"Guess what else was on the site, Sherry?" Stef says.

"The scoop on Dear Elle's diamond?" I feel my eyes go round like pizzas.

"A purse with a diamond clasp!" Lorraine says. "First time she's brought it out in public."

"It'll be beyond beautiful," I say.

Lorraine hitches her purse up on her shoulder, then mimes opening it as if it had a huge diamond clasp. The dog charm on her bracelet dances and glints with her movements.

"That bracelet is way cool," I say. "Is it your dog?"

"Oh no, I don't have a dog." Lorraine turns her wrist this way and that. "This is my absolute favorite piece of jewelry."

"Where'd you buy it?" I ask. "I wonder if they have any with a fish charm."

"They don't," Stef says.

"Did you get it near here?" I ask. "I could always check."

"She didn't," Stef says.

"Online?" I ask.

44

"No," Stef says.

What's the deal with the bracelet? Maybe Stef bought it as a gift for Lorraine. And maybe she got it for really cheap, and she doesn't want Lorraine to know.

Pasted on Junie's face is the look she gets when a math equation isn't working out right. "Let me get this straight. You guys only came here looking for Sherry?" She lifts her shoulders. "What made you think she'd be here?"

"Well, we knew from the magazine's website that the awards are at the Roosevelt tonight," Stef says. "So we guessed she'd stay in this hotel."

"And she looked super friendly in her photo," Lorraine says. "And we're down this way on Hollywood Boulevard a lot. So we took a chance and stopped by to say, 'Hey, job well done!'"

Junie's frowning, not really buying it.

It makes perfect sense to me.

"I just wish we could see you get your award." Lorraine sighs. Then she immediately claps a hand over her mouth.

Stef rolls her eyes. "Sorry, Sherry. Sometimes Lorraine opens her mouth, and we don't know what'll fly out." She glares at Lorraine.

Why shouldn't they come to the awards? They're my first fans. I bet Dad brought the envelope with the tickets. *Hollywood Girl* sent enough for my family and one for Junie. So Lorraine and Stef could use The Ruler's and Sam's.

"As it turns out, I have two extra tickets," I say.

"Uh, Sherry—" Junie starts to say.

I cut her off with a wave. I know the tickets are for friends and family. But if I lived here, I'd be great friends with these girls.

Lorraine and Stef gaze at me with big grateful eyes. "I could tell from your photo that you were generous," Lorraine says.

"More like crazy," Junie mumbles under her breath.

I only arrived in L.A. a few hours ago, and I'm already making friends and getting famous.

chapter
seven

I love a hotel room. It's like a mini life inside your real life. Makes me feel like I'm living in a snow globe.

Our room is very swank, with a soft beige couch, a modern silver floor lamp that resembles a tall science-fictiony plant, a totally tiled bathroom, photos of famous movie stars on the bedroom wall and a great view of Hollywood Boulevard, specifically Grauman's Chinese Theatre.

It's truly excellent that my dad's in his own room. His snoring is, in a word, scary. Plus, sharing a deluxe hotel room with my best friend means having a fancy slumber party every night.

We're getting dressed for the awards ceremony.

Junie's quieter than usual. Probably, she's still annoyed about Lorraine and Stef. Junie doesn't make friends as easily as I do. But, like I pointed out to her, she shouldn't be bugged about the free tickets. It took me two and a half seconds to hop the elevator up to our room, snag the tickets, then deliver them to Lorraine and Stef, who were sharing a soda in the hotel café. Plus, the tickets were trash if they didn't get used.

"But you don't know them," Junie says. "And this is a closed event with strict security."

"They're exactly like us." I pull my dress over my head. "Only fifteen and with tighter, shorter clothes and metal on their faces."

Despite Junie's moodiness, I'm still a complimentary friend and mention the loveliness of her turquoise + white paisley skirt and matching shirt. "Those colors really accentuate the different shades of red in your hair."

Junie stretches her lips taut like a monkey and brushes on wet shiny gloss. "Thank you." She smacks her lips together. "Your dress looks great, Sherry. The purple is really pretty." She drops the gloss in a tiny black purse. For touch-ups throughout the evening. "I hope this is a magical evening for you."

"Thank you." I give her a hug. My dress is actually violet, but I doubt Junie is currently open to correction.

I sprinkle mauve glitter in my hair, then twirl in front of the full-length mirror. My dress flares out with style and panache. Eat your heart out, Josh Morton.

From the hall, we knock on my dad's door. "Hurry up," I say. "It's time to go downstairs to meet our *Hollywood Girl* rep."

He emerges, dressed in tan. The Ruler's a big fan of the beige family and has redone my dad's wardrobe in the noncolor.

By the front desk, there's a tall and slim girl with long, flat, satiny blond hair and fake lashes that brush her pink cheeks. Her smile is megawatt. "Hi! Sherry Baldwin, right? I'm Madison Brown from *Hollywood Girl*."

She lightly grasps my shoulders and air-kisses either side of my head.

When I think of L.A., this is exactly how I imagine it. Streetfuls of beautiful people air-kissing.

"You look even more adorable in real life, Sherry." Madison leans toward Junie and air-kisses her. "So, you're the lucky best friend. Junie Carter, right?"

"Yes." Junie grins. "Is it okay if I take pictures? I'm the editor for our online school paper."

"Absolutely it's okay!" Madison says. "We're down with publicity at *Hollywood Girl*."

Madison gives my dad the air-kissing treatment too. He stands stiff and awkward, like he's one of the

Queen of England's soldier-guards, who, according to the Travel Channel, aren't allowed to talk or smile or show any expression. Even if you tell them a joke.

"You've got the tickets?" Madison asks my dad. "The policy this evening is 'no ticket, no entrance, no exception.'"

Junie shoots me a look, which I ignore.

Dad pats his suit pocket. "All in order."

Madison claps. "Yay. We're set."

Once she's herded us together mother-hen style, Madison ushers us to the ballroom. Along the way, she gives us the scoop on this evening's program. Like what's on the menu and how long the ceremony will run. She makes it sound fun, fun, fun. I'm particularly thrilled to hear that there will be an extravagant dessert bar.

"Dear Elle's really psyched about meeting you, Sherry." Madison beams at me. "She was blown away by the depth of your understanding of love."

"Yeah, well," I say. I'm really starting to feel like a fraud. I've had one boyfriend. The relationship didn't even last half a year. I'm no expert on true love. I'm more of an expert on short relationships that end with heartache and awkwardness.

"Sherry has always been emotionally mature for her age," my dad says. Then he jumps into a lame-o story of how I used to dress up my brother and push him around in my toy stroller.

Junie chimes in. "Sherry's really popular at school. She gets along with all the different cliques."

Thank you, Dad and Junie, for trying to make me look interesting and unique in front of Madison. But it's embarrassing.

The Blossom Ballroom has three tall medieval-style wooden doors. Only the middle door is open. A short, plump, spectacled man in a tux stands guard with an outstretched hand and a stern expression that says, "Either fork over a ticket, or go home."

"I'm Madison Brown, a *Hollywood Girl* staffer." Madison glances at his name badge while handing him hers. "Nice to meet you, Garrett."

"Uh-huh." Garrett rubs her badge between his thumb and forefinger, then locates her name on his clipboard. He's certainly not the friendliest man in the state.

Next, Madison gives Garrett our names. With a thin black Sharpie, he draws a slow *X* next to them, then reaches out for our tickets, which he checks übercarefully. Finally, in a low monotone, he utters, "Head table. Have a good evening." Hands clasped behind his back, Garrett steps to the side to let us pass.

This is serious security.

Madison leads us into the ballroom.

Junie and I gasp. My dad spins on his heels, exhaling a low whistle.

We have left the normal world of chores and homework and heartache. Hello, wild and wonderful fantasy world!

Overhead, the ceiling panels flash rainbow colors. Super-cute miniature windows line the room way high up, like we're in a castle. Round tables covered in crisp white cloths dot the large room. Everywhere, well-dressed, elegant people are chatting about their exciting lives.

From the back corner, a band rocks the party. A band with a strong drumbeat and boomy bass. A band whose tracks are on my iPod. A band Josh is crazy about. Camel's Breath!

Junie catches my eye. She recognizes the music too. She frowns and wags her finger at me as if to say, "Do not even consider going sad and weepy on your special evening."

Josh's mom drove him to countless coffee shops around Phoenix to listen to Camel's Breath before they landed bigger gigs. And now, here they are, opening for a *Hollywood Girl* awards dinner.

Josh. I sigh. My thumbs itch to text him.

Junie frowns and wags her finger at me again.

She's right. I squeeze my eyes until all I see is black. When I open them, the fantasy world with its lights and people and food smells floods in, filling me up. And Josh is gone. He's not ruining my evening. I won't let him.

Madison points to a table near the podium. "That's where you'll be sitting. There are name cards at each place setting." Then she points to a counter manned by another tuxedoed man. "Why don't you guys grab a drink and some appetizers? I'll catch up with you later."

She air-kisses me goodbye. "You'll hear me screaming for you, Sherry."

Junie's staring at the room through her camera's viewfinder. *Click. Click. Click.*

"Who's the band?" Dad asks me.

"Camel's Breath," I say. "They're pretty up-and-coming."

"Hmpf," he says. "I can think of some music that would really get this place hopping."

"Dad, Céline Dion is not the musical answer to all situations," I say.

Smiling, Junie snaps the cover back over the lens. "Those are some decent photos."

We head to the middle of the room, where there's a mountain of cheese with a bunch of different crackers, along with grapes and olives and mysterious little spreads. Not to mention other finger foods. We load up small plates, then hit the drink guy for a soda with a mini umbrella. I'm sniffing for my mother and keeping an eye out for Lorraine and Stef. Negative on both counts.

At the head table, we check for our names on

embossed cards with gold letters. On my right will be Dear Elle! On my left, Gloria Vasquez, a reporter for *Hollywood Girl*.

"Let's take a load off," Dad says. He can't wait to dig into his plate of high-cholesterol, trans-fatty snacks.

I'm sniffing for coffee. By the appetizers. By the drink bar. By our table. Where is my mother? I want her here for the ceremony.

"Sherry, are you getting a cold?" my dad asks.

Junie watches my face.

"Nah," I say to them both.

Dad bites into a drumstick. He chews slowly, savoring. "Deep-fried chicken. How I have missed thee."

My cell rings. "It's Paula. Across the miles, she can sense what you're eating, Dad."

He wipes his mouth with a napkin.

I put the phone to my ear. "Hi, Paula."

"Sam and I are calling to wish you good luck tonight," Paula says.

That woman has a memory like a steel trap. "Thank you."

"Make sure Junie and your dad take pictures. Maybe with their phones? So they can send them to us while the event is still going on. It'll be as though we're there with you."

"Sure," I say.

"Here's your brother," Paula says. "He wants to talk to you."

"Was I supposed to feed your fish today?" Sam asks.

"No! Not until tomorrow. Sam, do not overfeed Cindy and Prince. You'll kill them. The feeding schedule's on the fridge under the Pets Galore magnet." How can he be such a math brainiac, but incapable of following a simple chart?

"Hey, did you know I'm spending tomorrow night at Joe's?" Sam says.

"Sam, get Paula to help you with the fish."

"We're going cosmic bowling first," he says.

"Sam, listen to me. Do not let anything bad happen to my fish."

I hear The Ruler's muffled voice in the background.

Someone taps my shoulder. I turn my head. Yet another guy in a tux.

"Sam, promise me—"

"Break a leg, Sherry." Sam disconnects.

"Excuse me." The guy taps on my shoulder again. "Are you Sherlock Baldwin?"

"Yes."

"They need you at the entrance. There's a problem."

chapter
eight

★

"Hi, Sherry!" Lorraine and Stef say in unison. A little too brightly.

They're standing outside the entrance to the Blossom Ballroom.

"These two girls said you gave them tickets," says Garrett, the guard.

Lorraine and Stef are smiling way wide at me, their eyes pleading, "Help us. Don't leave us stranded."

"I did give them tickets," I say.

The girls relax.

"But their names aren't on my master list." Garrett holds up his clipboard.

"Probably the names Paula Baldwin and Sam Baldwin are," I say.

He runs a finger down the first page. "Yes, they are."

"Paula and Sam couldn't make it," I say. "And I didn't want the tickets to go to waste."

"Are these girls' names anywhere on my list?" He peers over his glasses at me.

"I doubt it," I say.

People in the line are grumbling. I'm starting to sweat. Garrett the Human Stop Sign obviously takes his job too seriously. Suddenly, I hear a cheerful, cheerleadery voice.

"Anything I can help with here?" Madison asks. "I need to get our guest of honor back to her seat."

"Guest of honor?" Garrett says suspiciously.

"Yes, Sherry Baldwin." Madison touches my shoulder. "You already checked her in."

"Hmpf. Your guest of honor is trying to sneak people in."

Madison looks at me.

"I didn't mean to sneak anybody in," I say. "I just gave my stepmother's and brother's tickets to Lorraine and Stef." I gesture at the girls, who are standing quietly, waiting for a verdict.

"These are your friends?" Madison asks.

I should say no. All I know about Lorraine and Stef is that they recognize a great essay on true love when they see it. And they dress cute and stylish. Tonight Lorraine's wearing black capris, a shimmery blouse and a black vest. Stef has on tight black leggings and a long fuchsia top. Both are rocking loads of gold eye shadow. However, Garrett's hard-core security-guard behavior is annoying to the max, and I want to get the girls in to bug him. Plus, I like them, and there's no reason for them not to attend. "Yes," I answer emphatically.

"Garrett," Madison says gently, "our guest of honor is allowed to invite four people. Her dad and one of her friends are already seated. Let's admit her other two good friends okay?"

Garrett steps to the side. "General seating only," he intones.

"We're in?" Lorraine says. She high-fives Stef. They skip around Garrett, give me a quick hug and disappear into the crowd.

Madison wraps an arm around my shoulder and gives a little squeeze. "Sorry about that." When we're out of earshot of the security guard, she says, "Garrett's brother is really high up in *Hollywood Girl*."

"No problem."

"Dear Elle is here and dying to meet you!" All that's missing from Madison is a pair of fluffy pompoms.

"I can't wait," I say. Walking through the room, I'm smelling for coffee. Nothing. Where is my mother?

When we get to the table, everyone is seated, including Dear Elle, who's chatting with the woman on her right side. The waiters have already served bread and salad. The Ruler would approve of the dark green leaves.

Madison pulls out my chair, and I slip in. "You're going to love her," she whispers. "I'm scooting over to my table. *Bon appétit.*"

"What was the big problem?" Junie asks me from across the table.

She would not approve of how I handled the ticket situation. "Nothing." I sip my soda. "Total misunderstanding."

"What did Paula want?" Dad tears off a chunk of his roll and slathers it with butter.

"To wish me good luck and ask you to text her pictures from tonight," I say.

Dear Elle turns to me, her blue-black hair glinting in the light. "Sherlock, it's so very exciting to meet you." She smiles at me while glancing around the table.

In real life, Dear Elle looks even younger than she does in the thumbnail photo in the magazine. Maybe early twenties. Her skin is completely blemish-free and wrinkle-free and freckle-free. She looks like a doll. And she's petite like me, about five feet one.

I'm gazing around, trying to find the purse. Junie's staring too. Probably already imagining the headlines.

From a silver hook clipped to the table, Dear Elle pulls off a black evening bag with a sparkling diamond clasp. "Girlfriends! Is this what you're looking for?"

I nod. Junie nods.

"That's the question I always get when I meet people. 'Where's the diamond?' " Dear Elle clasps and unclasps the purse so everyone at the table can see how it works. "Too cool, right?"

"Where do you get a purse like that?" my dad asks.

"This is a one-of-a-kind designer item. Made especially for me by Jake's Bags. It even came with this one-of-a-kind hook." Dear Elle hangs the purse back on the silver hook.

The hook is a cool accessory, but if I had an exclusive purse like that? I'd superglue it to my shoulder.

"Could I take a picture of you and your purse?" Junie says.

"Have we met?" Dear Elle swings the purse up by her face and smiles with small, sparkling teeth.

"I'm Sherry's best friend." Her eye peering through her camera's viewfinder, Junie pops off a few quick shots. "And the new editor of our middle school's paper."

"Sherry?" Dear Elle takes a dainty sip of water.

"Short for Sherlock," I say.

"That was a very good essay." Dear Elle trickles dressing from a silver jug onto her salad.

I feel myself blush. "Thank you."

"Have you read my book? *Love, Revealed*?" she says a little louder than necessary.

"Uh, n-no," I stammer. "But I follow your advice in

Hollywood Girl religiously. It's the first page I flip to when the magazine arrives in the mail. In fact, I can pretty much quote you word for word after a couple of—"

"I'll be signing after dessert," she interrupts. "And there are copies here for sale."

Gloria leans over me. "Dear Elle, I freelance for an entertainment paper that'd be interested in a book review and interview."

Elle flips her hair over her slender shoulder. "Awesome, Gloria."

"You have a lot of fans at Saguaro Middle School." Junie grabs a roll and passes the basket to the woman next to her. "They'd love to see pictures of you and Sherry together."

"Absolutely." Dear Elle pokes her fork into her salad. "And maybe a couple of poses on my own?"

The main course arrives. Dad digs into his steak like he hasn't seen one in months. Which he hasn't.

"Nothing like the aroma of a good steak, right, Sherry?" Dad says between bites.

In no time flat, the meal is over, including the chocolate fudge sundae and the lemon square I snag from the delicious dessert bar.

Dear Elle leans toward me. "Are you ready for your moment in the sun?"

I sniff. I guess my mother isn't going to make it. Bummer.

Junie pushes back her chair and pops the lens cover off her camera.

"But I don't have to talk, right?" I say.

"Just a few words. Nothing to get nervous about." Dear Elle pushes her straight hair behind her ears and brushes imaginary crumbs from her satiny blouse. "How do I look?"

"Great," I say. "But not a speech, right?"

"This crowd will love you, Sherry." She unclasps her purse and pulls out a tube. She reapplies blood-red lipstick. "Loosen up and go with the flow Dear Elle–style."

Going with the flow is so not me when it comes to class presentations, which seem totally tame compared with this evening. I snuffle in earnest. No coffee scent. I want my mother. Butterflies are fluttering and flapping in my stomach.

"If you need to blow your nose," Dear Elle says, "now's the time."

"I'm good," I say.

The band strikes up. Bright lights on stands are positioned at the front of the room. A couple of guys set up their cameras. Then, to a drumroll, a woman in a black pantsuit steps behind the podium. She introduces herself as the president of *Hollywood Girl* and spouts off the usual we're-glad-you-all-could-make-it junk. She gives out a few awards. Kudos to sales for selling stacks of *Hollywood Girl* in Europe.

The art department designed a cover that won something somewhere. Gloria Vasquez wrote an article that attracted a bunch of recognition in the industry.

The butterflies are basically hurling themselves around my stomach.

The clapping for Gloria dies down. "For the first time ever," the president says, "we ran a writing contest for our teen readers. We asked them to submit five hundred words on true love." She sips from a goblet of water. "We received many excellent entries. Many. But a certain entry stood head and shoulders above the rest." She looks over at Dear Elle. "And Dear Elle, our extremely savvy, extremely popular love advice columnist will tell you about the entry and introduce the winner."

"Please don't faint. Please don't faint," I repeat under my breath.

Amid thunderous applause, Dear Elle sashays to the podium, grabs the mic and proceeds to talk about her book. And her life as a writer. And then more about her book.

My stomach settles. The microphone is Dear Elle's best friend, and I am A-OK with this.

After many minutes, Dear Elle picks up a gold chain. A heart-shaped medal hangs from it. She dangles it in front of the audience. "Can you get a clear shot of this?" she says to the cameramen.

"Got it," one of them answers.

"Sherlock Holmes Baldwin—we call her Sherry—wrote an amazing essay on love. She totally owned the contest. *Hollywood Girl* is beyond thrilled to have her with us this evening." Dear Elle beckons to me. "Give it up for Sherry Baldwin!"

My dad's shrill two-fingered whistle slices through the applause. He perfected it at my brother's soccer games.

Like when you blend up all the ingredients of a smoothie, I'm a mixture of nerves and excitement. I stand and square my shoulders. I take a deep breath. This is my moment. I stride to the podium.

Dear Elle grasps my shoulders and does the air-kissing thing. I gaze out over the crowd. Many pairs of eyeballs gaze back.

Pushing up the corners of her mouth with her index fingers, Junie makes an exaggerated smile. As a reminder to me.

I paste on a grin and look around. Lots of faces grin back. My heart beats wildly. I'm a winner. A Hollywood winner.

"Sherry," Dear Elle says, cradling the heart pendant in the palm of her hand, "did you notice the diamond at the tip? Because, say it with me, people . . ."

"Diamonds are forever. Just like love," chants the entire room.

Dear Elle grabs my hand and lifts it straight up.

"Sherry Holmes Baldwin," she booms, "our teen love expert!" She drops my hand and starts clapping.

Thunderous applause. Flashing rainbow ceiling lights. Cameras on. I pinch my arms just to check that I'm actually awake.

Still applauding, Dear Elle hip-bumps me. "This group is digging you," she says out of the side of her mouth. "We're going with it."

"Going with what?" Suddenly, the butterflies are back in full nauseating force.

Dear Elle just shoots me a sparkly smile. When the room quiets down, she says in a loud voice, "You know what I want to hear?"

"What?" the audience shouts back.

"Whatever Sherry wants to tell us!" She starts clapping rhythmically. "Sherry! Sherry! Sherry!"

chapter
nine

A roomful of people clapping and yelling for me to make a speech?

Ack. Eek. Ike.

I thought grinning and gazing around would be enough.

There's a whoosh of coffee aroma. Mom! She breezes in next to me. "You can do this, Sherry. Pretend you're only talking to a few people. Start with thanking them for the award. And mention how much you enjoy reading the magazine."

Dear Elle nudges me toward the mic. I gulp in air.

"Say something," Dear Elle hisses in my ear.

The whole room goes all hazy and fuzzy edges for me. And it's like I'm up by the ceiling, looking down on everyone. Now I know what people mean by an out-of-body experience.

My mother stays beside me. I follow her suggestions. And once I open my mouth and start talking, most of the jitters disappear. I don't know exactly what I say, but I get a few chuckles and leave the podium with applause ringing in my ears. Not to mention my dad's whistle.

Then I'm seated and kicking back and enjoying the rest of the program. My brand-new shiny necklace dangles around my neck.

"You were amazing," my mom says.

I give her a thumbs-up.

Dad thinks I'm gesturing to him and gives me a thumbs-up. "Great speech, Sherry!"

"My mom rocks!" I mouth to Junie.

The rest of the event passes by in a blur. While Junie's snapping photos like she's a paparazzo and Dad's making multiple trips to the dessert bar, I manage to sneak to a corner for a chat with my mother. I press my cell to my ear so I don't look like a nutzoid yakking away to the air.

"Sorry I was late," she says. "I had trouble finding the hotel." When alive, my mother had no sense of direction either.

"You were there when it mattered," I say.

There's a light touch where she's squeezing my shoulders. "I am so proud of you, Sherry."

"It's pretty cool." I hold up the necklace, and the diamond sparkles.

After we've caught up a little, my mom says, "How much longer do you plan to stay?"

"A while," I say, looking at the line where Dear Elle is signing. "I'm going to buy Dear Elle's book."

"Really?" my mother sounds surprised.

"She is kind of a jerk, but she gives terrific love advice."

"Really?" my mother says, still sounding surprised.

Which doesn't surprise me. I mean, my mom is super at solving mysteries, but I doubt she knows much about love, especially for girls my age.

"If you're okay, I'm going up to the Hollywood sign to see if I can connect with Peg Entwistle's ghost."

"Peg Entwistle?" I say.

"An actress who died tragically in the 1930s. She jumped from the *H* in the Hollywood sign, back when it still said Hollywoodland," my mom says. "Word on the street is she and Marilyn Monroe's ghost are friends."

"Have they always been friends? Like even when they were alive?"

"No. Marilyn was only six when Peg died. But they were both very unhappy women who died under unusual circumstances. Apparently, they've reached out to each other in the afterlife."

"Well, I guess that's good," I say, not commenting on the incredible amount of weirdness.

"I've heard that Marilyn Monroe is hard to find, hard to get to, hard to get talking. I'm hoping Peg Entwistle is my in," Mom says. "I really want to get to the bottom of Marilyn's death. The foreign Academy would love me to as well."

Mom takes off, and I'm sticking my cell back in my purse when Madison shows up. "Sherry, people are really wanting to meet you! What a speech!" She hooks her arm around mine and marches me all over the room, introducing me to loads of magazine personnel and basically treating me like some kind of teen star. Finally, she leads me to the dessert bar, where we each choose chocolate swirl ice cream with toppings, then sit down at Madison's table to indulge.

Madison sets her spoon in the empty bowl and dabs at her mouth with a napkin. "Sherry, I have something for you." She digs in a bag under the table. "Here it is. Dear Elle's book. I have a copy for Junie too. Let's find her and then have Dear Elle sign them."

Junie's across the room, taking some wide-angle shots. She sees me looking for her and holds up her hand to signal "five more minutes."

Dad's near her, talking to a man in a suit. He finishes his conversation, then saunters over to me. "I'm ready to head back to the room, Sherry."

I hold up my book. "Junie and I'll be up after we get these signed."

"Fine." He turns to Madison. "Great evening. Thank you."

"I'm just so glad you could attend." Madison beams.

Walking across the room to the double doors, Dad loosens his belt.

There's a huge huddle around Dear Elle. Junie and I veer toward the end of the line.

"Sherry," Madison says, "you're a guest of honor." She approaches Dear Elle and taps her on the shoulder.

Dear Elle waves us to the front.

She signs my book, *To Sherry, a girl who truly understands love. Dear Elle XO*

"Junie," Dear Elle says, "could you forward any good photos you got of me to the magazine?"

Back in our room, I make a beeline for comfy sweats and the couch. Seriously, it's like getting home after a long vacation. Celebrity status, even for an evening, is exhausting.

Junie sits at the desk, boots up her laptop, and gets to work uploading photos and writing copy for the school paper while it's all fresh in her smart little head.

Dear Elle's book, *Love, Revealed,* on my chest, I'm stretched out, all mellow, half considering cracking open the book, half wondering why I bought the exclusive-to-*Hollywood-Girl*-readers-only Camel's Breath CD this evening. For Josh. I guess when you're dating someone, you get in the habit of noticing little things they like. Jazzed-Up Juice coupons, water polo key chains, Camel's Breath CDs. It's not like I *have* to give Josh the CD. But I might.

Junie jumps to her feet. "I can't believe it!"

I startle and bounce up. The book clatters to the floor. "What?"

She snatches the remote from the coffee table. "The news!"

"You practically gave me a heart attack for the news?" I pick up the book and lie back down.

Her finger dancing up a storm on the remote, Junie says, "I can't believe I got so into the school-paper stuff that I almost missed the news. That's really saying something. Like journalism might be my calling. And all these years I've been thinking astronaut." Channels whiz by at a dizzying speed. "At least the photos are uploaded. I just have to go through and delete the garbage ones."

Junie's been hard-core about the news since she was around five, only taking a brief hiatus when she got her tonsils out. Personally, I don't get it. Give me a decent reality show any day. That's close enough to the news for me.

I stand and stretch. "Are the Oreos in here or in my dad's room?"

71

"Oreos? You had three desserts!"

"Three desserts? Are you sure? I have zero memory of that. How scary. I wonder what else I ate. Vegetables? Liver? Pigs' feet?" I walk over to the mini fridge. "If I had to choose one word to describe tonight, it would be 'fog.'"

"Sherry! Quick!" Junie plops down on the couch. "This story's on the *Hollywood Girl* dinner."

I race over to the couch and plop down next to her.

The anchorman stares out at us. Above his left shoulder is a drawing of Dear Elle's diamond purse.

"So cute." I sigh.

"This evening *Hollywood Girl* hosted a gala event at the Roosevelt Hotel," a reporter says. "The event celebrated the accomplishments of various magazine personnel."

The screen fills with footage of the bald guy from sales marching up to the podium, then cuts to Gloria Vasquez giving her short acceptance speech.

Junie's and my head swivel toward each other. Am I going to be on TV?

"Dear Elle, the wisdom behind the popular advice column followed avidly by teens around the country, introduced the first-time teen winner of an essay-writing contest. The topic? True love, of course."

And there I am gliding to the podium. I look poised and cool. No way anyone could tell I was full of butterflies.

Junie and I scream.

"Your hair looks good," Junie says.

"But my dress!" I wail. "I had no idea TV did that to colors."

"The evening was not all glam and glitter," the anchorman continues. "Things soured sometime after dinner."

"What?" Junie and I say in unison. We sit up straight, shoulders touching, focused.

"Here's our Crime-Around-Town Reporter, Katie Scott. She was in the Blossom Ballroom at the Roosevelt Hotel a little before this newscast."

A slender reporter with glasses and a silver microphone stands at the wooden door. She raises the microphone to her mouth. "That's right, Paul. The atmosphere here in the ballroom changed from elation to outrage earlier this evening." She walks through the doorway and stands by the podium.

The room is mostly empty. Only a few members of the hotel staff remain, working on cleanup.

"At some point after dinner, someone at this extravagant affair stole Dear Elle's purse."

Junie and I gasp.

"Dear Elle is here with me," the reporter says, "and has agreed to answer some questions."

Dear Elle and the reporter are standing by our dinner table. The silver purse hook is still clipped to the table. Now, however, nothing hangs from it.

"When did you first notice your purse was missing?" The reporter tilts the mic toward Dear Elle.

"I didn't notice until I was gathering up my belongings at the end of the evening." Dear Elle runs her hand through her shiny hair. "At first, I just thought I'd misplaced it. But after scouring the entire ballroom, both on my own and with help, I finally came to the heartbreaking conclusion that my beautiful purse was stolen."

"There's something very special about this purse. Could you describe it for our viewers?"

"The clasp is to die for." Dear Elle places a hand over her chest. "Diamonds are a symbol of love. I'm a love guru. So every time I do a public event, I wear or bring something with a diamond." She touches an ear. "I've worn diamond earrings." She shakes a hand in the air. "Diamond rings. For this event, I brought an evening purse with a sparkly diamond clasp."

"When's the last time you remember seeing your purse?" Katie Scott asks.

Dear Elle stares off into space. "I opened it"—she talks with her hands, mimicking unclasping her purse—"pulled out my tube of lipstick and redid my lips." She draws in the air in front of her mouth. "That was just minutes before I went up to the podium." Dear Elle strokes her chin. "Then I pre-

sented the teen award to"—she tilts her head—
"Blaylock Baldwin."

"Blaylock?" Junie and I shout.

"I understand you were recently the victim of house theft?" the reporter says.

"Almost. I was out of town on a book tour." Dear Elle holds up a copy of *Love, Revealed*. "And my neighbor noticed some suspicious activity at my house and called the police. When they arrived, they found my back door open, but nothing had been stolen."

"How lucky," the reporter says.

"I'm not counting on luck anymore," Dear Elle says. "I had a super security system installed."

"You asked to say a personal word to our viewers. Would you like to do that now?" Katie Scott hands the mic to Dear Elle.

Dear Elle looks straight into the camera with big doelike brown eyes. "Whoever took this purse, this symbol of love, please return it." She pauses. "Diamonds are forever. Just like love."

A drawing of the purse fills the screen. A fat 800 number flashes across it, while the anchor's voice instructs all the viewers to keep an eye open and call the number with any leads.

A commercial for car insurance comes on.

I shake my sad little head. "I can't believe I was at

the scene and didn't have a clue that a crime was going down."

"Did you see anything weird?" Junie asks.

"Nothing. I was in a cloud. A celebrity cloud. I'm the girl who doesn't recall scarfing down three desserts."

"I can kind of remember the purse hanging on the back of her chair when she was signing." Junie's eyes are closed while she tries to re-create the scene.

"The thing with purses is that you pick them up, set them down, take stuff out of them, shove stuff into them. All on automatic pilot." I twirl a few strands of hair around my index finger. "Dear Elle could easily have unhooked her purse, thrown it over her shoulder and carried it to the signing table. All on autopilot."

"Like my mom and the garage door," Junie says. "She always thinks she forgot to close it. But every time we go back, it's closed."

Junie and I sit in silence. A commercial for a new camera comes on.

We snap to attention.

Thanks to Junie, we have about a million shots of the evening. Maybe even one of the thief stealing the purse.

chapter
ten

Junie zips to the desk, grabs her laptop and hustles back to the couch.

We huddle side by side, eyes on the dark screen coming to life.

"Where are our minds at?" I say. "That we didn't think of your photos?"

"Seriously." Junie presses a bunch of buttons. "I pretty much chronicled the entire evening."

"Wow, Junie." I gape at her gajillion thumbnails. "That's a boatload of photos."

Junie starts scrolling. "I got a new memory card for the trip."

I touch the screen. "Stop there." I'm looking at

several photos, practically identical, taken almost right in a row.

"Yeah, I was practicing with the sports mode. Where I hold down the shutter release button and pop off a bunch of shots fast." She points to me on the screen. "Like here. I'd moved away from the table, so I had a clear view of you. I held down the shutter button and started clicking to make sure I got you on the way to the podium."

"Aw, thanks." I squint. "So, at the side of these shots, you caught Dear Elle pulling the purse off the hook and opening it. Then you missed part of the sequence."

"Sorry. I was trying to find a different place to kneel, I think," Junie says. "My focus was on you, not on Dear Elle redoing her makeup."

"In this picture"—I tap Dear Elle's mouth—"her lips are all red. So she's finished with her lipstick."

About ten more shots in, a photo shows the handle of the purse hanging from the hook.

Then there are several shots of me pushing back my chair, walking to the podium, talking. A few good ones, a lot that need to be trashed forever. I point out one particularly ugly picture where I'm leaning toward the crowd, distorted beyond belief, with a nose longer than Pinocchio's. "Can we delete this now?"

Junie sighs. "We'll go through them later." She

scrolls some more. Then there's a ton of photos of the signing.

"So, you took these from off to the side of Dear Elle?"

"Yeah, I was trying to get different perspectives."

"There's Lorraine and Stef in the line. I didn't realize they ended up so far behind us."

Junie pushes her glasses up her nose. "Here's Dear Elle signing and looking up at a girl. Actually, that's a pretty good profile of both of them." Junie pats her own shoulder. "Now there's a gap because I changed location."

Sure enough, the next batch of photos are taken from behind the signing table. The purse is in the corner of the picture, hanging lopsidedly over the back of Dear Elle's chair.

"She must've left the hook at the table where we ate," I say.

Next come several blurry shots of the line. Maybe from people jostling Junie.

Then Lorraine's at the front of the line. She's smiling and chatting with Dear Elle. That girl is so friendly.

A girl about the width of a spaghetti noodle is on Lorraine's heels. "What happened to Stef?" I ask.

"No idea," Junie says. "It's weird behind the lens. I'm in my own little world. I get pictures and don't have a clue about all the details until later. I never noticed Stef was missing."

The next shot is of Lorraine crouching low to the table and leaning in close to Dear Elle. Lorraine's finger is on a sentence in the middle of the book. The book is at an angle, so that the print isn't upside down for either of them. Dear Elle's head is cocked, and she's squinting at the print. Her mouth is half open as she explains something. Not an attractive look.

"Wow. Lorraine said she didn't read," I say, "but here she's asking a question about something way far into the book."

Weirdly, Lorraine is not looking at the page, but past Dear Elle. It's a nice close-up shot of an author and a fan, except that the fan doesn't seem to be tuned in.

Four panoramic views show people around the room and in the line. Still no Stef.

Next, the skinny spaghetti girl steps toward the table, shoulder blades jutting out from a low-cut black dress.

And then I see it—or actually, I don't see it!

I think I've figured out the sequence of events for how the purse got stolen. The bottom of my stomach drops out.

"Junie, pull up the photo of Lorraine and Stef in line together. Next to it, drag in the photo of just

Lorraine at the front of the line. Third, put the photo where Lorraine shows Dear Elle the sentence or whatever in the book. Fourth is the spaghetti girl walking away."

"I'll play it as a slide show," Junie says.

"Keep an eye on the lower corner," I say.

The loop plays over and over. Dear Elle's purse dangles over the back of her chair while both Lorraine and Stef are in line. It's still dangling when Lorraine is waiting her turn. Lorraine and Dear Elle bending over the book fill the photo, so there's no way to tell what's going on with the purse. But by the time the skinny girl's approaching Dear Elle, Stef and the purse have disappeared.

Lorraine and Stef stole the purse.

And I helped them.

chapter
eleven

The next morning, Junie bounds out of bed and throws open the curtains. The sun is shining bright and cheerful.

This is the opposite of my dark and gloomy mood. I tossed and turned all night. In the harsh bathroom light, I look like a football player, with unattractive black lines underscoring my eyes. And I have the beginnings of a headache.

While smearing on triple layers of Naked Makeup's Cover-Up Supreme, I mull over recent events in my life. Like scratching at a scab. I practically handed Dear Elle's purse to Lorraine and Stef. They read my essay and the details of the awards dinner on the *Hollywood Girl* website, guessed I'd be at the

Roosevelt Hotel, flattered me and tricked me into getting them into the dinner. Where they nabbed the purse. Pretty embarrassing.

There's a knock at our door. "Good morning, girls," Dad booms. "Rise and shine." He knocks again. "I've already been out to pick up hot chocolate and doughnuts."

Hot chocolate and doughnuts? He's really living life on the edge.

The second she's settled in the living room with a cardboard cup of hot chocolate + whipped cream + shaved chocolate and a doughnut with strawberry icing + sprinkles, Junie switches on her computer.

"Did you catch any of the news last night, Dad?" I ask.

"Just the sports." He pats his stomach and picks up a shiny cruller. "I think I have a little corner reserved for this guy."

Junie slurps, then starts click-clacking away on her keyboard.

"Dad, remember Dear Elle's designer purse with the diamond clasp?" I say. "Someone stole it from the awards dinner. The story was on the news."

"Was anything else stolen?" He sets the box of doughnuts on the coffee table. "Any other purses? Wallets?"

"I don't think so." I flip open the box and pick out a chocolate doughnut.

83

"Whoa." Junie looks up from her screen. "There've been lots of home burglaries in Beverly Hills lately, and some people think the theft of Dear Elle's purse is related."

She sets her computer next to the doughnut box, and we all crowd around.

Did the Beverly Hills Bandits Strike Last Night?

Detective Tatiana Garcia, Beverly Hills Police Department, has been working overtime, trying to crack the case of the Beverly Hills Bandits, a person or group of persons responsible for breaking into celebrities' homes and stealing millions of dollars in big-ticket items, as well as trinkets and clothing.

Detective Garcia insists the department is close to making an arrest. Beverly Hills celebrities aren't buying it. Recent victims Melanie Grace and Owen Gordon admitted to late-night talk-show host Jay Leonard that they and their famous friends feel targeted and want police to be more aggressive in shutting down the Bandits.

A few weeks ago, an attempt to rob Dear Elle's Beverly Hills home was abandoned when neighbor and good friend Hannah Smyth, of Dancing with the Stars fame, noticed an unfamiliar van in

Dear Elle's driveway and notified police. Officers arrived on the scene minutes after the van left. When questioned, Ms. Smyth stated, "That van was totally the wrong color for our street. I knew something wasn't right."

Then, last night, during <u>Hollywood Girl</u> magazine's gala event at the Roosevelt Hotel, Dear Elle's designer purse with a diamond clasp was stolen.

Detective Garcia is collaborating with the detective at the Los Angeles Police Department who's handling the purse theft. The fear? That the Beverly Hills Bandits are evolving into the Bandits Without Borders.

"So, Lorraine and Stef are involved in burglarizing stars' homes?" Junie chooses a jelly-filled doughnut.

I rub my temples, which now pound rhythmically, like a metronome. "Yikes. They are some kind of bad."

"Who are these girls?" my dad asks.

"You might have seen me talking to them last night? They were dressed almost identically in black capris and black vests—"

My dad cuts me off with a shake of his head. "Sherry, I didn't notice what anyone was wearing. Well, except you two, who were the belles of the ball."

Junie and I roll our eyes.

"I have incriminating photos of those girls on my camera," Junie says.

"More like circumstantial evidence." I explain to my dad about the sequence of the photos.

He bites into his cruller and chews thoughtfully. After swallowing, he says, "I want to take care of the rental car this morning. So why don't I go do that right now while you two get ready for the day? Then we'll drive over to the police station with Junie's pictures."

"I call first shower." Junie is already logging off.

"Does anyone have Tylenol?" I ask.

Junie and my dad shake their heads.

"Give me a sec to throw on my shorts, Dad," I say, "and I'll go down to the lobby with you. I bet they have Tylenol in the gift shop."

Minutes later, when I'm a couple of footsteps into the elevator, I smell coffee.

The door glides closed on me and my dad. "Meeting by the pool," my mom says in my ear. "To discuss last night's theft."

My breath catches in my throat.

"Mrs. Howard is here," she continues. "Don't worry. She just wants to touch base."

Mrs. Howard, my mother's guidance counselor at the Academy of Spirits? She has a Southern accent, can be as mean as a pack of eighth-grade girls, smells like cinnamon rolls when pleased and like burnt sugar when annoyed. My heart sinks faster than the descending elevator.

The elevator doors open and I shuffle toward the gift shop. When she knows the whole scoop, Mrs. Howard is going to eat me alive.

"Sherry! Sherry!" my mom says.

I tune in. "Huh?"

"I didn't say anything," my dad says.

"The pool's not that way," my mom says.

I press my palm against my forehead.

"You'll feel better after you buy that Tylenol," Dad says.

"Oh, you have a headache." Mom gently lifts my hair. "I'll let Mrs. Howard know you'll be a few minutes late." The smell of coffee disappears.

Before we part ways, Dad says, "We'll hunt down Detective Garcia as soon as I get back with a car."

"Sure. Sure thing." I plod down the hall and into the hotel gift shop. I can't believe I just rode in an elevator with my dad and my ghost mom. And didn't think about how bizarre it was, especially given that my dad is totally oblivious to my mom's presence. And how awkward is it for my mom that my dad is remarried? Plus, I forgot to tell my dad to rent a cool car. I am definitely überworried.

I'm staring at the shelf, trying to find Tylenol, when I feel eyes on me. A cute guy about my age with

87

straight dark hair, dark eyes and a SOCCER ROCKS! T-shirt nods in my direction. My pulse quickens, which I do not understand because I am so not over Josh.

I pay for a bottle of water and the Tylenol. As I'm leaving the store, I can't stop myself from glancing over my shoulder to see if the guy's watching me. He is.

Then it's down the hall, through a door leading to the back of the hotel property, past a tiled fountain, and onto a walkway to the pool area, where my mother's waiting for me.

"How bad's your head?" my mom asks.

"I'll be okay." With my finger, I push a couple of Tylenol to the back of my tongue, then wash them down with a swig of water.

The pool sparkles in the morning sun. Tall palm trees reach for fluffy cotton clouds. I wend my way past chaise longues.

"She's over in the corner at the back. At the table between the palm and the fire pit," my mother says. "Sherry, don't be nervous. Everything's fine."

Easy for her to say. She doesn't know about my connection to Lorraine and Stef.

The closer we get to Mrs. Howard's table, the stronger the smell of cinnamon buns gets, until it's cloying and overly sweet. I'm barely seated in a white plastic lawn chair, when a round fuzzy shape hovers above me, fluttering the table umbrella. "Hiya, Sherry. Are you aware of what's being said about you?"

Mrs. Howard rarely wastes much time on chitchat. I stay silent. She asked what's called a rhetorical question, meaning if you try to answer it, you'll just make things worse.

"I am sorry to report that the World Wide Web for the Dead is filled with the news that you were present during a robbery. Let me share some of the headlines: 'Is it a coincidence that the mother-daughter duo were at the *Hollywood Girl* reception last night?' 'Were they supposed to prevent the heist?' 'Are they losing their touch?'"

The fuzzy round ball that is Mrs. Howard expands and grows darker. I can make out a furrowed brow and a dark slash of eyebrow. "Remember, Sherry, when I talked to you about the responsibility of being associated with this here Academy? I emphasized how our enemies would be constantly on the lookout for y'all to fail."

"Yes," I squeak.

"Well, I am just appalled and dismayed at how these ghosts are chasing after you, trying to tarnish your good reputation. They are like hound dogs on a false trail," she says. "Of course you had nothing to do with last night's robbery. You're honest and quick-thinking. An asset to our Academy."

"Oh," I say. Guilt is like a noose around my neck.

"I represent the entire Academy," Mrs. Howard drawls, "when I apologize for the behavior of these sensationalist-seeking ghosts."

The noose of guilt tightens.

"I have issued a statement claiming you are not even acquainted with the two thieving teens." Mrs. Howard places a blurry hand on her blurry heart. "I want you to comprehend how much I believe in you."

I'm choking.

"And this extends to you, too, Christine," Mrs. Howard says.

"Actually," I say, "Mom was barely at the event, just long enough to be a good mother and see me get the award. She definitely wasn't around when the robbery happened."

"You know when it happened?" Mom and Mrs. Howard say together. And I'm sure their ghost jaws drop.

I tell them about Junie's photos.

"You *might* know when it happened," Mrs. Howard drawls. "Those photos don't sound overly conclusive. But I agree with your decision to take all this to the police."

"On the news, they said they were close to wrapping up a mystery dealing with celebrity break-ins," I say. "The detective made it sound like Dear Elle's purse was part of that case."

"Glad to hear they're on the brink of solving it," Mrs. Howard says, "because the Academy of Spirits will be taking a hands-off stance with all of this." She sinks her large blurry self into the chair across from me.

"Our online experts advise us to ignore the Internet hubbub and let it die a natural death," Mrs. Howard continues. "Reminds me of duck hunting. The dogs flush out a flock, and there's a flurry of quacking and flapping and shooting. Followed by silence."

"How did the girls gain admittance to the dinner? Wasn't it by invitation only?" my mom asks, morphed into detective mode.

I swallow. "Well, actually"—I draw the word out as long as I can—"I got them in."

I confess all the sordid details.

Mrs. Howard bloats up like a poisonous puffer fish, ready to pop and spew all over the place.

chapter
twelve

My father does not return with a dorky rental car. *Au contraire,* he returns with a very cool convertible! It's silver with black pinstripes and a black top, which will always be down if I have any say. This is the best thing that's happened to me today.

As we're tooling out of the hotel parking lot, my dad floors it. This is the second best thing that's happened today.

Junie cinches her seat belt.

"Wow, Dad," I say, "I didn't know you had it in you."

"You should've seen me back in the day. I was the man with my souped-up cars." He squeals into a tight right turn onto Sunset Boulevard.

So different from The Ruler and her tentative-grandma driving style, white-knuckled hands gripping the steering wheel at ten and two. I smile. I'm loving our father-daughter bonding!

We zoom down Santa Monica Boulevard, a warm California breeze and exhaust from other cars blasting across our faces. If Junie tightens her seat belt another notch, it'll slice her in half.

My dad looks over at me and winks. "This is the life." He grinds into the next gear. "Wind in your hair. Doughnuts in your gut. And a car that hugs the road."

I should be following my dad's lead—letting loose and living it up in Southern California.

But the ugly poolside scene earlier shook me to the core. Mrs. Howard was furious. The most furious she's ever been. She wants to kick me out of the Academy.

Even though she's angry with me too, my mother talked and pleaded and argued with Mrs. Howard. Bottom line: I'm on probation. My orders are to hand over the photos from the *Hollywood Girl* event to Detective Garcia. To lie low and not call attention to myself while the detective cracks the case. To make sure my behavior doesn't land me on the World Wide Web for the Dead.

My eyes fill up. I can't be fired. I love working with my mom. I love solving mysteries for the Academy.

His grin as wide as the road, Dad is zipping in and

out of traffic. He pops in a Céline Dion CD. He's so happy and carefree. Like a real person, not just a father.

A siren wails.

Lights flash behind us.

It's a police car!

My dad pulls over to the curb, kills the engine and rolls down his window.

"Sir, do you realize how fast you were going?" says the police officer, his double chin bobbing.

"Not exactly," my dad says.

"Sixty-five miles per hour," Junie says.

I glare at her.

"Yep. Sixty-five is what I clocked you at. And you're in a construction zone."

Dad groans.

The officer reaches out a beefy hand. "Driver's license."

Dad fumbles with his wallet, trying to slide his license out from where it's stuck in a little plastic pocket. "Baked in by the sun," he mutters. He's frowning the whole time. Sixty-five miles per hour? In a construction zone, which means an added penalty. He's an accountant and knows the value of money.

The officer eyes the license. "Arizona?"

"Yes, Officer," Dad says. "We're here for five days. My daughter won a trip to Hollywood through—"

"I'm gonna run this." The officer waves the license in the air and lumbers back to his car.

Dad rubs his forehead. He doesn't look so happy and carefree now.

Junie's phone beeps with a text. She reads it and a smile plays around her lips. Must be Nick. She's immediately thumbing in a response.

The officer marches back. With his teeth, he pulls the cap off a pen and balances a thick pad on one palm.

"You know, Officer," Dad says, his voice higher than usual, "we're actually on our way over to your home away from home, the Beverly Hills PD. To fulfill our civic duty."

The officer raises a bushy eyebrow.

"Yes, that's correct," Dad continues. "We attended a fancy dinner last night at the Roosevelt Hotel. An evening put on by the *Hollywood Girl* people. These two"—Dad jerks a thumb at us—"figured out who stole the purse with the diamond clasp, and they have photos to show the detective in charge."

"Is that right?" the officer says. He couldn't sound more bored without being asleep. "Half the country seems to think they can solve this case." He scribbles out a ticket, then tears it off the pad and hands it to Dad. "Have a good day."

Like there's a possibility of that happening.

We crawl the remaining distance to the police station. Seriously, any slower and the engine will choke and die. A deep line creases Dad's forehead. Probably he's imagining sharing the details of this escapade with The Ruler.

Junie loosens her seat belt and is a happy and relaxed passenger. She and Nick are texting up a storm. Each ping is a stab to my heart, a reminder that Josh and I will never text again. At one point, Junie even chortles. She is oblivious to my pain.

I'm about to point out that she's wasting her vacation with her nose stuck to her screen, when Junie stops grinning and texting, shoves the phone in her purse and slings her camera case over her shoulder. It's journalist time.

From the street, the Beverly Hills Police Department looks like a Spanish-style church. We nose slowly into the covered parking lot. Dad parks carefully between the white lines. He's definitely back to being a dad.

The three of us walk through the parking lot and up a cement ramp to double glass doors trimmed in turquoise. The sign above reads POLICE DEPARTMENT.

"Here's some Beverly Hills trivia," Junie says. "No one is born or buried in Beverly Hills because there are no hospitals or cemeteries."

Once inside, we approach the counter, which is surrounded by glass. Probably bulletproof glass.

We wait while the police officer behind the counter finishes sorting through papers in a wire basket. He moves the basket to a low shelf. When he straightens up, I can read his name badge. Officer Mullins. He's short, with unruly hair and a belly like a shelf. He reminds me of a penguin.

"Excuse me," I say. "Did you guys recently move?"

He shakes his head. "Why?"

"With all the turquoise accents, the staircase and your little protected area, it doesn't look even close to the police station in the *Beverly Hills Cop* movies."

"Not one of those movies was filmed inside our station." His voice, filtered through a mic, is tinny.

Gazing around, I nod. I knew something didn't add up.

"What can I do for you, folks?" the officer asks.

Dad leans his chin in toward the mic in the glass. He clears his throat. "Well, my daughter here, Sherry Holmes Baldwin, is somewhat of an amateur sleuth. A successful amateur sleuth." He pats my shoulder. "We're very proud of her."

Ack. This is so embarrassing.

Officer Mullins smiles at me, the way you smile at someone's poodle. "She's too young for a ride-along"—he shuffles around under the counter—"but we do have some coloring books somewhere."

"We're not really into coloring books, but thanks." I take over for my dad. "Actually, we're here because

97

we have some important information about the theft of the purse with the diamond clasp at last night's *Hollywood Girl*'s gala."

"Oh yeah?" He opens a small door in the glass and slides through a pad of yellow lined paper and a pencil. "Jot it down, and I'll get it to the detective in charge of the case."

"I think Detective Garcia would be very interested in the photos we took at the dinner," I say.

"Detective Garcia doesn't have time to meet with every person who wanders in here with a lead," Officer Mullins says. "You go through me first. That's the process."

Junie holds up her camera case. "I shot the photos with this digital single-lens reflex camera. I used one of the sharpest lenses available. Great pixel density." She starts to veer into even more detail, like counting photons and diffraction.

Officer Mullins looks to my father for help.

Dad shrugs. "Teenage girls." He shoots a quick, secret wink at Junie and me. "They have more staying power than you or I."

"Let's see the pictures," the officer says.

Junie turns on her camera and tilts it toward him so that he has a view of the small screen. She starts clicking through last night's shots while I give a running commentary.

"I've seen enough." He picks up the phone. "A couple of teens and their dad are here with photos of the *Hollywood Girl* gig. I'm not sure there's anything of interest." He listens. "You *do* want to see them?" He hangs up. "Go up to the third floor, then follow the signs to the Detective Division."

chapter
thirteen

We climb the stairs, hanging on to the cute turquoise banister. We walk along the hall, passing a restroom and a door with TRAFFIC DIVISION above it. At the end of the hall, there's another officer sitting behind yet more bulletproof glass.

Before I have a chance to introduce myself, the door next to him opens and a woman in uniform bursts through. "I'm Detective Garcia." She's got her hair pulled back in a ponytail and is wearing adorable pink lipstick.

We introduce ourselves.

Detective Garcia eyeballs Junie's fancy camera. "Come on back and show me what you've got." She's very down to business.

We follow her past clusters of desks and tall filing cabinets. Officers talking on the phone or writing notes glance at us, but not much more than that.

At the back of the room, Detective Garcia stops at a super-messy metal desk littered with Reese's Peanut Butter Cups wrappers, a few open cans of soda, several file folders and a brand-new shiny desktop computer. At my house, Detective Garcia would not be getting her allowance.

Nonchalantly, I glance at the sticker on the top folder. The Beverly Hills Bandits!

"The pictures?" Detective Garcia prompts.

Junie turns on her camera.

Personally, I believe a story is best told from the beginning. I take a breath. "I wrote an essay on true love for *Hollywood Girl* magazine. Surprise of all surprises, I won."

"So, you're the Blaylock Dear Elle mentioned in her news interview," Detective Garcia says. "I thought you said your name was Sherry."

"*Sher*lock. Sherry, for short," I explain. "Anyway, I won a trip to Hollywood for me, my dad and a friend, which is why Junie and her camera were at the awards dinner."

"I'm taking over as editor for our online middle-school paper," Junie adds.

Detective Garcia makes a hurry-up signal with her hand.

Junie taps a couple of buttons, then holds the camera up so the detective can view the screen. "These two girls, Lorraine and Stef, are in line to have Dear Elle sign a book. In the lower right-hand corner, right here"—Junie points at the screen with her pinkie—"you can see the purse." Junie forwards to the next photo.

"And in the second shot," I say, "only Lorraine is in line. Then, here in the third shot, Lorraine's showing something in the book to Dear Elle. But she's not even paying attention to Dear Elle. She's looking over her shoulder at someone. Who? It must be Stef."

"And then I snapped this fourth shot at the same angle as the first shot," Junie says. "Here's where the purse should be hanging. It's gone."

"The purse is only in the first two pictures of this scenario," Detective Garcia says. "There's no way to tell when it was stolen."

"I think"—I blow out a breath—"looking at the photos this way doesn't give you the sense of timing we have as bystanders who were actually at the signing table." This is not a cop who thinks outside the box, who sees possibilities and shades of gray. This is a black-and-white-thinking kind of cop. I have a sinking feeling.

"Apparently not," the detective says dryly. "But there's an undefined amount of time for when the purse could have been lifted. Not to mention it could've been taken by someone who was never in the signing line."

"My daughter has somewhat of a reputation as an amateur sleuth," my dad says, trying to help out.

The detective sighs. "And the woman who was in here an hour before you said her tea leaves told her the purse is on a boat with yellow markings."

"But Sherry has actually *solved* mysteries." Dad's eyes flash.

Detective Garcia stares at her desk and waits, like she's counting to ten. "Look, Mr. Baldwin, there are only so many hours in the day. My best bet is to follow the strongest leads. The two teens in these photos aren't my strongest leads."

What started out as a sinking feeling morphs into a we're-dead-ducks feeling. I have less and less faith this detective will crack the case. I know Lorraine and Stef stole the purse. But Detective Garcia's totally dismissing their involvement. I can't have this mystery hanging like a dark cloud over my reputation with the Academy.

Why did I have to get Lorraine and Stef into the awards dinner? My first Beverly Hills fans? More like my first Beverly Hills felons.

Detective Garcia turns to Junie. "Those are all the photos from last night?"

"Uh, no." Junie grins. "There's a couple hundred more."

The detective's eyes bug. "And they're here, stored on your camera?"

Junie nods.

"I'll upload them to my computer." The detective reaches for Junie's camera.

Junie pulls it closer, like a favorite stuffed animal. It's instinctive. She doesn't like people messing with her stuff, especially her electronic stuff. It's sort of an only-geek-child behavior.

"This is a good camera," she says. "Which I bought with my own money. And which I need for taking pictures for our school paper."

"Okay." Detective Garcia chews on her lower lip. "Maybe we can compromise."

I blink. Detective Garcia thinks Junie wants to trade the photos for insider info about the case!

The detective chews off what's left of her cute pink lipstick. "We've narrowed the ringleader of the Beverly Hills Bandits down to two suspects. I want to examine your photos to see if either of them attended the event."

"So you're sure the same person is responsible for the celebrity break-ins and Dear Elle's purse?" I ask. "The MO is so different."

Her eyebrows raised in a subtle question, Detective Garcia stares at Junie.

Junie unzips the side pocket of her camera case and pulls out a cable.

"For connecting the camera to my computer?" says Detective Garcia, palm up.

"I'll do it," Junie says. Sharing is definitely not that girl's strong suit.

"What MO are we talking about?" My dad is blind to the delicate negotiations taking place between Junie and the detective. Actually, I think Junie is blind to them too; she's just safeguarding her camera.

With her cable, Junie attaches her camera to the detective's computer.

"The MO. The modus operandi. No, obviously, it isn't the same," Detective Garcia says. "The Beverly Hills Bandits break into the homes of young celebrities. Celebrities about the same age as Dear Elle. In fact, Dear Elle is friends with some of the victims." Detective Garcia leans over her computer, pressing keys to start transferring JPEGS from the camera to the hard drive.

"On the news, they were saying that someone tried to burglarize Dear Elle's house but got interrupted and didn't get anything," I say. "Still, why target her purse? I mean, it's cool, and it's probably worth a bunch. But not compared with all the things you can steal from another house. Plus, stealing the purse in front of everyone was risky."

"Actually, there are two hundred fifty-three pictures," Junie exclaims, watching the computer screen. "Who knew I was so shutter happy?"

"Two hundred and fifty?" The detective sighs. "Fine. This is not for general consumption." She pauses. "At every break-in, a key is stolen. Usually a house key. The thief never uses the key to break back in at a future date. It's more like a souvenir. The burglar didn't get a key from Dear Elle's house. Last night, the thief got his souvenir. Dear Elle's house key was in her purse."

A boring old house key as a souvenir? That doesn't sound like Lorraine and Stef.

My dad's cell phone rings. He pulls it from the pouch clipped to the waistband of his jeans and glances at the screen. "Work. I'll take this outside." He leaves.

Detective Garcia flips open the top file in the middle of her desk and pulls out two head shots. "Were these men at the dinner?"

The two suspects! The first guy has a long, thin face, wavy hair combed off his forehead and wire-rimmed glasses. The second has eyes spaced closely together, flared nostrils and Dumbo ears.

Junie and I both shrug. "The ballroom was packed," I say.

"Just because he doesn't look familiar doesn't mean I didn't get a picture of him." Junie knots her cable and zips it up in the case with her camera. "There are several crowd shots. You can zoom in on your computer because of the high resolution of my photos."

"Garcia," calls a detective from a desk behind a row of filing cabinets. "Ya gotta sec?"

"What's going on, Bowen?" she calls back.

"I got an informant on the phone who only speaks Spanish. Come translate."

"Sure." Detective Garcia jogs to the middle of the room.

I make a snap decision. "Junie, quick! Turn your camera on!" I open the Beverly Hills Bandits' folder and set papers out on the desk.

"Sherry! Put those back!" Junie's eyes go wide.

I grab the camera case out of Junie's hand, unzip it and yank out the camera. Then I'm turning it upside down and sideways, trying to find an On/Off button.

Junie grabs it back.

"This cop can't see that Lorraine and Stef are involved. She's never going to wrap up the case," I whisper frantically. "I'm solving this mystery myself so I get off probation with the Academy."

Junie frowns at me.

"Please," I say. "I'll owe you big."

"Fine." In a flash, the camera's on and Junie's squinting through the viewfinder. "I'm going to hate myself for this."

As she clicks, I scoop up papers, then lay out fresh

ones. I even set out the two head shots, then flip them over so Junie can snap the names. I'm concentrating and trying really hard to put everything back in the folder exactly the way it was.

We're totally focused on the contents on top of the desk.

Überly focused.

"Girls, what are you doing?"

It's Detective Garcia!

chapter
fourteen

My back hunched over and shielding the desk, I sweep the last few papers back in the folder. Then, standing tall and straight, I slap my hands on my hips and an attitude on my lips. Offense is usually the best defense. "Detective Garcia, were you trying to erase all the data off Junie's memory card?"

"What? No, no, not at all." Flustered, the detective pushes flyaway hairs off her forehead. "Did I really do that?"

"Yeah, well, we spent a bunch of time recovering pictures for the school paper," I bark. "Plus, my dad's in the parking lot and texting us to hurry up. I've already spent enough of this year grounded."

The detective tugs open the drawers of her desk. They're overflowing with crinkled papers and clips and pens and Reese's Peanut Butter Cups. "What if I make you a CD of the photos from my computer?" She rummages around in the mess. "I don't understand how I erased data. It's a new computer, though, and I'm not a techie."

"Uh, it's okay. I got it, uh, figured out," Junie says. She's not as quick and spontaneous as me in a tricky situation. She bundles her camera up and tosses the case strap over her shoulder, all set for a quick getaway.

"Are you sure?" The detective's still poking around her desk. "Someone here will have a blank CD."

"All is saved," I say.

Junie and I skip out of the Detective Division. Then we barrel down the stairs to the exit.

My dad's leaning on the metal rail outside the door, Velcroing his cell back in his belt holster. "Girls, now that we've got that chore out of the way, it's time for a little tourist fun."

Junie perks up. Running risks and breaking the law do not agree with her. Even in the best interests of a case.

Personally, I'm not up for fun. I'm on probation with the Academy of Spirits and I want off. Detective Garcia and her ineptness can only worsen my situation. I have to solve the case of the Beverly Hills Bandits. Before it's time to return to Phoenix. Nope, no fun for me. I'm totally in detective mode.

"Actually, Dad, I'd like to head back to the hotel room. Maybe take a nap." Maybe scroll through Junie's two-hundred-plus photos looking for Detective Garcia's two suspects. Maybe examine the pages from the file that Junie took pictures of.

He punches me lightly on the arm. "Not happening, pumpkin. When is the next time you, Junie and I will be in Los Angeles? Maybe never."

"Unfortunately, I think I'm suffering from jet lag." I fake yawn.

Dad bursts into laughter. "Good one, Sherry. 'Cause everyone gets jet lag from the ninety-minute flight between Phoenix and L.A." He laughs again. "If nothing else, our family has a great sense of humor." He struts off down the walkway to the parking lot, gesturing for us to follow. "Come on, girls."

Unblinking, Junie stares at me and says evenly, "You. Owe. Me."

I grab her hand. "Let's go play tourist!" For five minutes.

Over his shoulder, my dad's outlining our schedule. He ends with a pat to his jeans pocket. "I have the discount tickets Paula found online for Madame Tussauds wax museum."

We pile into our rental and cruise cautiously back to the Roosevelt, where we ditch the car and amble out to Hollywood Boulevard.

To be accurate, Dad and Junie amble. I'm more like sprinting, practically galloping. The sooner I get to Madame Tussauds, the sooner I'm out of Madame Tussauds and on the case.

"Sherry!" Junie calls. "Come back!"

My dad whistles.

I pull a U-turn and retrace my steps, huffing and puffing.

In *Star Wars* heaven, Junie's posing between two street performers in costume: Darth Vadar and Chewbacca.

"Stand beside me." Junie's voice is high and excited, like a little kid's on Christmas morning.

I squeeze between her and Darth Vadar.

"Smile," Darth Vader commands in a scary, deep voice.

I give a quick grimace.

"Uh, Mr. Baldwin, you're holding my camera upside down," Junie says.

She's letting my dad touch her camera? *Star Wars* has fried my best friend's brain.

"I know. I know. Just tricking you." Dad turns the camera right-side up and shouts from behind the viewfinder, "Okay, girls, say 'Céline Dion.'"

"Smile," Darth Vader commands again.

Chewbacca grunts and drapes a hairy arm over my shoulders.

At that very second, standing in the bright sun on a California sidewalk with my best friend and a couple of nutzoids in *Star Wars* costumes, I make a decision. I'm going with the flow and enjoying the afternoon with my dad and Junie. It's like the Lazy River at the water park, where it makes way more sense to float around and hang with your girlfriends than to swim against everyone and wind up kicked and dunked and yelled at. The mystery can wait a couple of hours.

Dad tips the street performers. We continue on our merry way, hamming it up with various characters like Batman and Mickey Mouse. Junie snaps several shots of my dad play-swordfighting with a pirate.

She also takes about a million photos of the sidewalk. Because we're on the Hollywood Walk of Fame and strolling right on top of big five-pointed brass stars that are embedded directly in the cement. There are five categories of stars: television, motion pictures, live theater, recording and radio. The celebrities' names are in the center of the stars. We pass a star covered in wreaths and flowers because the actor recently died.

Madame Tussauds is a total blast. The wax figures are so lifelike, it's as if you're really hanging with these famous people. Except, of course, they don't talk or change expressions, and they feel gross. Anyway, we're surrounded by movie stars, Hollywood icons, even sports stars, which really thrills my dad. Junie's camera continues to get a major workout.

"Gotta go, buddy." Dad pats Lance Armstrong on the shoulder. "I'm starving."

"Me too," Junie says. "But I'm definitely coming here again to do the behind-the-scenes stuff. Like making a cast of my hand and learning more about Madame Tussaud's life and how she sculpted for the French king Louis XVI. What great newspaper articles those'll be." She's so excited, her freckles stick out all 3-D.

Back on Hollywood Boulevard, we stop at a hole-in-the-wall Mexican restaurant next to a tattoo parlor. The chips are warm and salty; the fish tacos are delish, with the perfect amount of cabbage; and the churros are sweet and cinnamony.

"Hey, Dad, why don't you run next door and get a tattoo for dessert?" I giggle. "You know, surprise Paula."

"Very funny," he says, reaching into his pocket for his ringing cell. "Hello." He listens. "Really? No kidding?" His eyes are bright. "Let me check with the girls, and I'll call you right back."

"What's going on?" I ask.

"That was the client I'm meeting with tomorrow

morning. He wants to take me to the Comedy Store this evening. I'd have to leave you girls at the hotel, but you could order room service and rent a movie."

"Go for it, Mr. Baldwin." Junie unrolls her taco and spoons salsa into the middle of it. "Sherry and I can entertain ourselves."

"Maybe you can pick up some new jokes while you're there," I say. My dad is the king of groaners.

The three of us meander over to the Roosevelt. Dad's jabbering a mile a minute, trotting out sad knock-knock joke after sad knock-knock joke. Junie's polite chuckle is wearing pretty thin by the time we hop over Eddie Murphy's star and into the hotel. I've rolled my eyes so many times, my headache's coming back.

The afternoon was fun. Buckets of fun.

But it's time to buckle down and get to work on the case of the Beverly Hills Bandits.

Time to examine those illegal photographs of Detective Garcia's file.

chapter
fifteen

$\mathbf{S}$eated at the desk and sharing a wide square chair, Junie and I stare at her computer. She uploaded all the photos from her camera of the papers from Detective Garcia's file.

"This is a list of the burglaries with names, addresses, dates and times." I'm running my finger down the screen. "Melanie Grace, Jocelyn Dixon, Hannah Smyth, Owen Gordon. Wow. It's like a mini tour of hot young Hollywood stars." I look at the dates. "That's a lot of burglary for a little under half a year."

Junie clicks to the next photo. "Notes on a suspect named Cameron Williams."

I read.

```
Suspect: Cameron Williams
Address: 863 Mollison Ave. Apt. G, L.A.
Crime: burglarized 3 homes in Beverly Hills
for electronics.
Prior convictions for vehicle theft and
petty theft.
Chino State Prison: served 3½ years of
5-year sentence, released early 6 months
ago for good behavior.
Current Status: on probation.
Employment: 5 months at Taco Magnifico,
799 Upchurch St., L.A., 24-hour restaurant,
works night shift. Manager reports suspect
takes home his free tacos, naps during
lunch, keeps to self, always on time.
Notes: 2 Beverly Hills residents said
suspect looked familiar and thought they
had seen him in the area within the last
6 months.
```

On the hotel notepad, I jot down the addresses of Williams's home and Taco Magnifico.

Junie pulls up the photo of the next page from the detective's folder.

It's general notes about the case.

```
Beverly Hills Bandits
1. Victims all in their early twenties,
more female than male victims.
```

2. Either no or very simple security at the residences.

3. Most break-ins at night.

4. Some victims have pets. The dogs are small, with a few that fit in a purse.

5. A variety of high-end merchandise was stolen (electronics, jewelry, watches, designer purses, artwork) as well as personal items of little worth. The personal items have not shown up on eBay or at local pawnshops.

6. All the victims use the same pool company: Sparkling Pool Service & Repair, 227 N. Fairfax Ave., L.A. Owner: Derek Rizzo.

I add the contact information about the pool company to my notes.

"In that online article, Detective Garcia said the police were close to making an arrest." Junie messes with her screen so that it's brighter. "Do you think it's true?"

"No way," I say. "Cameron Williams looks suspicious because he committed a similar crime in the same area and has maybe been spotted there since getting out of prison." I squeeze out of the chair and grab our bag of snacks. "And the break-ins started around the same time he got out. But that doesn't mean he's definitely one of the Beverly Hills Bandits."

"Thanks." Junie opens a roll of Life Savers and pops a red one in her mouth. "And just because all the victims have their pools cleaned by Sparkling Pool doesn't necessarily implicate the manager or other employees."

"There's lots of detecting still to do on this case." I pick through the candies until I find a green one.

Next, Junie pulls up the list of items stolen.

There are two lists: a long column of high-ticket stuff and a shorter column of personal items. Items with the words "sentimental value" beside them rather than a dollar amount. Like a locket with a baby picture, a dog dish handmade by the owner, a Hard Rock Cafe T-shirt.

"Junie, you won't believe this!" I point to the screen.

Under "personal items" is "a silver bracelet with a dog charm."

Junie's shaking her head. "Lorraine and Stef are definitely involved."

Next, we pull up the head shots and names of Detective Garcia's suspects. The thin-faced guy with glasses is Cameron Williams. The guy with flared nostrils and big ears is Derek Rizzo, manager of Sparkling Pool. We painstakingly compare the suspects' head shots with each and every photo Junie took at the awards dinner. By picture #253, it feels like we went to the beach, scooped up fistfuls of sand and rubbed it in our eyes.

And the detective's suspects are not in any of Junie's photos. Which doesn't prove they weren't there. It only proves they were never in front of Junie's lens. It certainly doesn't prove they weren't involved. Maybe Lorraine and Stef were paid to lift the purse.

"Detecting makes me thirsty." Junie flips open the room-service menu and scans it. "Let's get smoothies."

Smoothies remind me of Jazzed-Up Juice. And Jazzed-Up Juice reminds me of Josh. And Josh reminds me of heartache. I'm not healed enough to order a smoothie. Probably I'll have gray hair before I drink my next smoothie.

After one look at my face, Junie changes her order. "I'm more in the mood for nachos and soda."

This is why you never let a best friend go. They're totally on your wavelength.

While waiting for our food to arrive, we talk over tomorrow.

And how we're tracking down an ex-con.

chapter
sixteen

An ex-con.

I've never met one. I've never questioned one. I've never searched for one.

But tomorrow I'm doing all three.

Who can sleep with that on their mind? Not me. It's two o'clock in the morning, and I've probably gotten one whole second of shut-eye.

Junie is übercranky if she doesn't get her required ten hours. No way I can face an übercranky Junie *and* an ex-con. So I quietly push back the covers, throw on some clothes and grab a room key and my purse.

I tiptoe into the dim hall, past the photos of movie stars lining the walls, and ride the escalator down to the lobby level. The hotel café, 25 Degrees, is open all night. The name stands for the number of degrees difference between cooking a medium-rare versus a well-done hamburger. This is the kind of trivia you pick up when you hang around Junie.

Entering the restaurant, I blink in the fluorescent overhead lights. The room is long and narrow, with tables and chairs along one side and a counter with stools along the other. The wall behind the counter is a wild silver and black diamond pattern. The tables all have a view of Hollywood Boulevard through a wide rectangular window. The place is empty.

"Grab whatever table you can find open," the only waiter says. "Or you can sit at the counter."

Oh great. It's two o'clock in the morning and I have to stumble across a waiter with the same sense of humor as my dad.

I slide along a red leather bench and pick up the plastic menu. "I'll take a turkey burger, fries and a soda." A turkey burger is a sign of The Ruler's influence.

Then, basically, I just sit there alone in the bright, quiet restaurant and fret. About how I've disappointed Mom and Mrs. Howard. About how I have to solve this mystery to get off probation. About how the case is like a big jigsaw puzzle when you first open the box and dump out the pieces on the table. I'm still at the stage of turning the pieces picture-side up. I haven't even connected the corner pieces yet.

After delivering my meal, the waiter disappears into the back of the restaurant.

I chomp down on my burger and chew. Whatever degrees they cooked it at, it's good.

I'm chewing away, then sipping on my soda, fading in and out of my thoughts, just letting the mystery rattle around in my brain, hoping pieces will hook together.

Suddenly, I hear crying. I glance around. The restaurant is dead. No other customers. No waiter in sight. "Hello?"

The crying gets louder.

I scoot out from my bench seat, then peek under the table next to me. Nada. More crying. "Hello?"

And then I smell it—Lippy's Root Beer Gloss. The scent's coming from two booths away.

I've found another ghost!

I check to make sure the waiter's still in the back, then whisper in the direction of the root-beer-gloss scent. "Who are you and what's the matter?"

The ghost hiccups. "You can see me?"

"Uh, no," I say. "But I can hear you, and I can smell your lip gloss. I used to be totally in love with that brand."

"This is the first time in a whole year"—her voice catches—"that anyone has noticed me."

My heart clenches for her. "Who are you?"

"My name's Leah Jones. I'm thirteen years old. I died in a horseback-riding accident."

"Thirteen? I'm thirteen too! You died at thirteen? That's horrible!" I can't even imagine dying at my age. It seems so unfair. Poor Leah. "When did you die?"

"A little over a year ago."

"I'm really sorry." I move back to my own table, and the scent of Lippy's Root Beer Gloss follows me.

"Did you ever see the movie I was in? It's called *A Horse Named Charley*." Leah's voice comes from across the table.

I shake my head. "I've never heard of it."

"I was the neighbor. Not the largest part, but a stepping-stone."

The door behind the counter opens. The waiter peeks out, playing cards in his hand. He looks over at me. "I thought I heard talking. Maybe another customer?"

"Just my phone." I hold it up as proof. "I'll let you know if you get any new customers."

"Thanks." He waves his cards in the air. "For once, I'm up on the chef at Texas Hold'em."

I wait till the door closes. "I'm Sherry Baldwin." I squirt ketchup over the fries. "So, why were you crying?"

"I cry every day. I'm lonely and sad. I don't know

how to get out of the hotel, and I've been stuck here ever since my death."

"I think learning to cross thresholds is a typical problem."

"How do you know?"

I tell Leah about my mom and how she had a tough time with thresholds.

"I miss my family and my dog. And I had the worst last day," Leah says with a sob, "because my boyfriend broke up with me. Right where you're sitting."

I shift a couple of inches. No need to encourage more bad karma in my life. "And that's why you're still at the Roosevelt?"

"I guess." And I'm sure she's shrugging. "You've probably heard of him. Michael Throck."

I choose a fry and nibble. Michael Throck! Yuck. That actor is constantly in the entertainment news. His nickname is Sox Throck because he changes girlfriends as often as he changes his socks. "You've been crying over him for a whole year?"

"One year, three months and twenty-seven days. To be exact."

Ack. Eek. Ike. I so do not want to feel sorrowful and grief-stricken over Josh by this time next year. "I Googled for ghosts at the Roosevelt. And your name didn't pop up. I wonder why." I take a bite of my burger.

"I didn't show up in a Google search?" Leah wails. "I'm never going to be famous."

"What other ghosts live here?" I ask. "Maybe Google is totally inaccurate for the spirit world."

"There's an old guy on the ninth floor, Montgomery Clift, who plays the bugle sometimes," Leah says. "And occasionally I hear Marilyn Monroe's voice coming from the mirror she haunts."

"My mom will be ecstatic to hear about Marilyn Monroe," I say. "She's determined to get to the bottom of her death."

Leah sniffs. "Have you ever been dumped?"

Suddenly, there's a lump in my throat. I nod.

"Do you want to talk about it?"

And, surprisingly, I do. Maybe because it's late and I'm tired and stressed. Maybe because Leah is a stranger and it's a brand-new story for her. Maybe because I miss Josh and I just want to talk about him. When I'm finished spilling my gloomy guts, I wipe my nose with a napkin.

"We have a lot in common," Leah says. "You should get insomnia every night, come down here and we'll cry our eyes out about our broken hearts."

I sit up straight. "No, no, no. I do not want to do this every night. I don't want to be sad and depressed. I want to get back to being my normal self." I think briefly about how much my mother has accomplished in her year and a half of death. "Leah, you've wasted enough time moping over Michael. You need a hobby or something. Seriously. It's time to move on."

"Like you should be giving me advice?" Leah's voice drips with sarcasm. "What exactly are you doing to get over Josh?"

"I'm solving a mystery."

There's a long and awkward silence. I know Leah's still at the table because the root beer smell is strong. I keep on eating my burger and fries. I said what I believed, and I don't have anything to add.

"Sherry," Leah says when I'm on my last delicious bite, "thank you for being so honest."

I slurp the last drop of my soda.

"You're absolutely right. I need to look around, get outside myself, get involved in other stuff. I need to stop dwelling on Michael."

My mouth full, I give her a thumbs-up. I do love it when people listen to my wisdom.

"So, I'm on board. You have a crime-fighting partner. Me."

Ack. Eek. Ike.

chapter
seventeen

The next morning, Junie, my dad and I eat breakfast across the street. I manage to sneak out of the
hotel without bumping into Leah. I'm not up for a
ghost shadow.

"I'm so hungry," my dad says, "I could murder this
bowl of cornflakes. Does that make me a cereal
killer?" He slaps his knee and busts up.

It's going to be a long day. I yawn.

"Sherry, come on. At least crack a smile," my dad
says. "My delivery was perfect."

"Was the Comedy Club good?" I halfheartedly
spread grape jelly on toast. I'm still pretty full
from the burger and fries I chowed down only a few
hours ago.

"Amazing." Dad dumps a packet of sugar in his coffee. "I'm thinking I should try a routine at open-mic night at the Comedy Spot in Scottsdale when we get back home."

Junie looks at me.

"Will you be using a fake name?" I take a mini bite.

He laughs. "You are a chip off the old block, Sherry. Quick with the witty comebacks." He pours in so much half-and-half that his coffee turns a light, light tan.

After breakfast and many bad bacon-and-egg jokes, Dad heads off to his business meeting. Junie and I take a taxi to 863 Mollison Avenue, apartment G, home of Cameron Williams. Ex-con.

"You girls live here?" the taxi driver asks.

"Uh, no," I say, handing him money. "We're, uh, visiting people."

"This isn't a nice neighborhood." He counts back our change.

No kidding. An ex-con lives here.

"Stay together. And walk out to the main road to find a taxi," the driver adds.

Junie watches him drive off and gives a little shiver. "I don't have a good feeling about this."

We start across the potholed parking lot and up the cracked walkway to the two-story apartment complex. I hop over a flower struggling to grow through one of the cracks. Trash litters the dirt on both sides of the walkway.

A boy roughly Sam's age whizzes out from the gap between two buildings. He's going about a hundred miles per hour on a bright and shiny skateboard. The skateboard comes to a dead halt when it hits the dirt. The boy flies off and lands next to an empty In-N-Out Burger cup lying on its side.

Junie and I rush over. "Are you okay?" Junie asks.

He jumps up. "Of course. I'm tough. Like a super-hero. A skateboarding superhero."

"Do you know where apartment G is?" I ask.

"Yeah." He flips his skateboard right-side up.

"Do you know the guy who lives there?" I say.

"Yeah."

"What's he like?" I say.

"He's a really good skateboarder."

"What else?"

"That's all. I can't think of anything else."

"How about tacos? Does he like tacos?"

"No." The boy spits in the dirt. "He's so sick of tacos."

"Very odd," I say to Junie. "I'm questioning Detective Garcia's skills more and more."

"Where's apartment G?" Junie asks.

"Follow me." The kid hops on his board and disappears down the alley between the buildings.

By the time we get there, he's nowhere in sight. We

walk along, looking for letters on the unit doors. Some have letters; some have shadows where the letter fell off and the paint underneath is less faded. Most of the wooden doors are open, which means we have to go up close and peer for a letter through the screen door. Sounds from inside the apartments carry out to us: commercial jingles on TV, dishes clattering, voices.

We round another corner. And there's the boy, standing on a stoop, arms crossed. The skateboard is propped up against his bare leg.

"We thought we'd lost you forever," I say.

He stretches out an arm. "Welcome to apartment G. Pleased to meet you."

I slap my palm against my forehead. I can't believe I didn't see that coming. It's so eight-year-old boy.

"But you're not Cameron Williams," Junie says.

"Oh." His face falls. "You're looking for my uncle."

"And you," I say. "What's your name anyway?"

"I can't tell you." He frowns at me like I'm an idiot. "You're a stranger." He picks up his skateboard, opens the screen door and shouts, "Uncle Cam! Some weird girls are here to see you!"

A man in a faded T-shirt and ripped jeans shuffles to the doorway. He's balancing a drooling baby dressed in pink on his hip. Even with huge circles under his eyes, he's easily recognizable as Detective Garcia's ex-con suspect, Cameron Williams.

"Can I help you?" The baby squawks and he shifts her to his other hip.

"Hi, I'm—" I pause and count to three before spouting off the name of a burglary victim, "Melanie Grace." I watch Williams closely for a reaction, but he looks blank. "And this is my friend . . ."

"Jocelyn Dixon." Junie pronounces each syllable slowly and distinctly.

"Are your names supposed to mean something to me?" he asks. "Because they don't."

The boy is sitting on his skateboard, riding up and down a neighbor's stoop. Each time he bounces down, he squeals.

"Stop, Alexander," Williams says. He turns to us. "And why are you here?"

I smile wide and phony. "We're volunteers with the American Blue Cross."

Junie's trying to copy my wide and phony smile, but she ends up looking more like a chimp.

"Blue Cross?" Williams frowns. "You mean Red Cross?"

"We're like the Red Cross"—I smile ever wider, to the point of pain—"but we volunteer less often and do fewer good deeds. You know, like once in a blue moon. That's probably why you haven't heard of us."

Junie launches into an explanation of a blue moon. She literally can't help herself in these situations. It's like she's overflowing with trivia, and it just leaks out her mouth. Especially when she's nervous.

The baby starts kicking her legs and screeching.

Poor Junie is forced to stop with the blue moon facts. She manages to squeeze in, "We can expect about fifteen blue moons over the next twenty years."

"Does that mean I can expect to see you girls volunteering fifteen times over the next twenty years?" Williams smiles.

"Uh, no," Junie says. "Those facts are independent of volunteering." Apparently, she left her sense of humor in Phoenix.

I laugh loud enough for two people.

Alexander is back to thumping his skateboard on the stoop. That kid's nonstop energy. Worse than Sam.

"Alexander, come inside for cartoons." Williams rubs his eyes.

When the boy ignores him, Williams adds, "You can have a sucker."

At the sound of that sweet news, Alexander stands and tucks his skateboard under his arm.

Williams pulls a rag from his jeans front pocket and swipes at the baby's drool. He opens the door. "Come on, Alexander. We're all going in."

Ack. We haven't even started our questioning.

"Do you realize the fire department considers this complex a high-risk area for fires?" I babble.

One foot ready to cross the threshold, Williams turns back and looks at me. "Really?"

"Seriously, like one of the worst. Everything here could blaze to ashes"—I snap my fingers—"like that."

Alexander drops his skateboard to the pavement and jumps on it.

"That's why the, uh, American Blue Cross sent us to talk to you about fire prevention," Junie says.

"If you're looking for donations, you're in the wrong neighborhood." The baby pulls on Williams's hair. "Most people will be tapped out until the beginning of the month."

"No, no," Junie says. "We don't want money."

The baby starts screaming. I tickle her tummy. She goes completely still and gives my gold hoop earrings a long, appreciative stare. A girl is never too young to enjoy decent bling. She reaches out her chubby arms for me.

"Can I hold her?" I say. "I'm good with babies."

"Sure." Williams looks relieved at the break. He passes me the baby, then the burp rag. He shakes out his arms like he's been hanging on to her for hours.

Junie's face scrunches up at the sight of the rag. She takes a step away from me and the baby. She will never be a popular babysitter.

Our best bet for keeping Williams out here and getting him talking is if he doesn't have to focus on the kids.

"Hey, Alexander." I raise my voice. "I have a brother your age. Eight, right?"

Alexander makes a face like I just force-fed him broccoli. "I'm nine! My birthday was yesterday. And my party was at Dave and Buster's, right, Uncle Cam?"

Williams nods. "That was quite a party, wasn't it, buddy?"

"Uncle Cam won over a hundred tickets. I bet you can't do that."

Williams was at Dave and Buster's yesterday? When? For how long? It takes a while to win a hundred tickets. I make a talking gesture with my hand at Junie. As in, now's the moment to trot out your precious fire-prevention trivia.

She looks blank, then straightens her shoulders. "So, when was the last time you changed the batteries in your smoke detectors?"

"You must have printed material, right?" Williams says. "Why don't you give me that and I'll read it in my spare time."

"I'm so sorry," I say, all exaggerated sad. "We already gave away every last flyer. But Jocelyn has the information totally memorized."

Holding the baby close, I walk over to Alexander.

"I absolutely could win over a hundred tickets. I rock at games," I say. "I've had a birthday party at Dave and Buster's too."

"We stayed a really long time. Even though it was expensive. I bet your party didn't go that long."

"Probably not." I sit down next to him and bounce the baby on my knees. "Who went?"

He reels off a bunch of names, ending with his mom and his Uncle Cam.

The baby twists and turns in my arms, trying to get down. I sit her next to me and let her play with the zipper on my purse.

"Was your Uncle Cam there the whole time?"

"Yeah, just my mom had to leave. She's a waitress at Sloan's." Alexander flips over his skateboard and starts spinning the wheels with the palm of his hand. "And she can't miss any more days or her boss will fire her."

"Bummer."

"Not really. Uncle Cam let us stay until closing. Which is one o'clock in the morning." His eyes flash with excitement. "My mom never would've done that. Plus he gave me this skateboard."

"Very cool. Does your uncle work at Sloan's with your mom?" I ask, just to check Alexander's reliability.

He shakes his head. "Taco Magnifico. The worst job, because he brings home tons of free tacos for us." He fakes throwing up. "I'm sick of them."

"Who babysits you?" I ask. "They could feed you mac and cheese or hot dogs, right?"

Alexander shakes his head. "No babysitter. Uncle

Cam watches us during the day. My mom's home at night."

I don't think Cameron Williams has time to get involved with the wrong side of the law. What with looking after his nephew and niece during the day and working the graveyard shift at Taco Magnifico.

Williams would probably fall asleep in the middle of a heist. Also, he definitely has an alibi for last night, when Dear Elle's purse was stolen. He was bringing home extra tacos to feed the family. So they're obviously hard up for cash. Am I one hundred percent sure Cameron Williams is aboveboard? No. But I'm sure enough.

I tap the top of Alexander's head. "Why aren't you wearing a helmet?" Once a big sister, always a big sister.

I walk over to Junie and Williams. I hand him back the baby. "You should cut way back on Alexander's sugar intake. As in, don't give him candy. I'm speaking from personal experience."

I yank on Junie's arm. "Let's go."

"I was just getting into carbon monoxide," she grumbles as I wave goodbye.

chapter
eighteen

It's after lunch. Junie and I are standing in front of Grauman's Chinese Theatre. To the left of us is Madame Tussauds.

"In about fifty years, they're going to run out of concrete blocks for hand- and footprints," Junie says.

I'm sniffing the air, trying to catch the scent of coffee. "I am so excited. My mom and I have talked about this place for years. And now we're finally here. And together. Well, in an überweird sort of way."

"You're not going to mention the mystery, right?"

Ack. "Absolutely not. My mother would make me promise to stop working on it. She'd make me follow Mrs. Howard's rules because she doesn't realize how lame Detective Garcia is. And how I'll never get off probation if I'm counting on that detective."

"Text me when you're going back to the hotel," Junie says.

"You're sure you don't want to hang with us?" I uncap my lip gloss for a quick touch-up.

"You two need some mother-daughter time." Junie pulls out a pen and notebook from her backpack. "I'm collecting info from the wax museum for an article." She takes off.

I stare at the tall theater. It's like a Chinese pagoda, with two red columns, wrought iron masks and a dragon above the doors. People laughing and joking in a bunch of different languages jostle past me. They pose and take pictures. We're all happy to be in Hollywood, thrilled to check out how our hands and feet match up to those of the celebrities.

The strong smell of coffee wafts toward me. I want to break out in a tap dance of joy.

Hollywood! Movie stars! Me! My mother!

"Hi, Sherry," Mom says. "Where's Junie?"

"Madame Tussauds." I scrounge around in my purse for my phone, then clamp it to my ear so I don't look like a whacked-out crazy person carrying on a conversation with herself. I really need to save up for a Bluetooth. "Junie's doing this in-depth article for the school paper about making the wax figures." I shake my head. "I'm not sure she really has her finger on the pulse of middle-school students."

"Oh, I'd give her some credit. She's a pretty smart cookie," Mom says. "Something I'd like the three of us to do is a tour of the stars' homes. Junie could write about that for the paper."

"Sounds great," I say.

Mom brushes my hair behind my ears. "Sherry, how are you doing? Mrs. Howard was pretty harsh at our meeting by the pool."

"She was hateful." I'm scrounging in my purse again, this time for gum.

"She takes her job very seriously. And she's not used to dealing with teens," Mom says. "You're following her rules, right? I want you off probation. I probably have one more assignment with the foreign Academy, then we could be working together again."

This is tricky. I don't want to lie, but I can't exactly tell the truth. "We gave the photos from the *Hollywood Girl* evening to Detective Garcia. Junie actually uploaded them onto the detective's computer." I pop a strip of gum in my mouth. "And I'm being really cautious in everything I do."

"Great. I know it's only a matter of time until the detective clears up the case. Then this whole mess will blow over, and we'll be back to business as usual."

I chomp hard on my gum, chewing words about the

detective's abilities into my molars. "How'd it go at the Hollywood sign with Peg Entwistle?" We're walking along the uneven stones of the theater's forecourt, dodging the other tourists.

"Very interesting." My mom's voice speeds up with excitement. "Peg is sure Marilyn Monroe's ghost will make an appearance in the mirror at the Roosevelt's Marilyn Monroe look-alike party on August fifth. It's also the anniversary of her death. There's bound to be lots of people there. And Marilyn always loved a crowd."

"In the meantime, she's just wandering around L.A. by herself?" I say. "She must be lonely."

"*If* she's by herself," Mom says matter-of-factly. "Marilyn had men falling all over her when she was alive."

I balance in Hugh Jackman's footprints.

"I would love to talk with her," Mom says. "Imagine solving the mystery of Marilyn Monroe's death, the mystery of the century."

"Well, if anyone can ask her the right questions and get her to answer them, it's you, Mom." My mother was a fantastic detective with the Phoenix Police Department. She caught tons of criminals.

So strange that we're both intent on solving mysteries this trip. Mysteries to do with famous people. But different mysteries and different famous people.

We're by the front doors of the theater. The theater that hosts the premiere of many movies. I tingle all over.

"Look! Look! Look!" Mom's squealing with excitement. "Marilyn's stone!"

"We gotta see how I measure up to her," I say.

We wait while people snap pictures of their feet and Marilyn's feet. Of their hands and Marilyn's hands.

Finally, it's my turn. I crouch down. "Wow. Mom, my hands are almost as big as hers. And I'm still growing."

"Do you see the broken rhinestone dotting the *i*?" Mom asks.

I run a finger over its rough edge.

"Marilyn wanted a diamond inlaid in her signature," Mom explains.

"Of course, because . . ."

"Diamonds are a girl's best friend," we say in unison.

"Sid Grauman wouldn't go for a diamond, but he did have a rhinestone put in," Mom continues. "It took only three days for someone to try to dig it out."

I trace Marilyn's loopy signature.

We find stones for lots of other celebrities. It's like Christmas morning for us. I take a couple of photos with my phone and send them to Brianna. She texts me back: <thx. Babysitting sux>

From the gift shop, I buy a ticket for the Chinese

Theatre tour. At the end of the tour, I ask the guide to take a phone picture of me in front of the theater's wooden doors. My mother's floating next to me.

The photo's kind of grainy because my phone's camera isn't the best. But if I squint hard, there's a little part of my shoulder that's missing, where my mother might have her arm around me.

I send the photo to The Ruler's phone for Sam. My brother won't notice where my mother's hand might be resting on my shoulder. He doesn't know about my mother's life at the Academy of Spirits or about the contact I have with her. He can't smell her coffee scent or talk to her the way I do. But when she's around him, he feels safe and good like he did when she was still alive. I want him to have this photo.

"Hard to believe the theater's over seventy years old," my mother says.

"That's old." My phone rings. "Hey, Dad."

"Hi. Just touching base. I'm still with my client. What are you and Junie up to?"

I fill him in. We make plans to meet up later.

I hold my phone against my ear, take a deep breath and ask my mom a question that's been on my mind for a while. "Mom, is it sad for you to see Dad? I mean, he's remarried and he's kind of got the same life you two used to have. But now you're not part of it."

"Hmmm . . ." And I can just imagine my mother sitting the way she always did, one leg crossed over the other, her foot drawing little circles in the air while she considers her answer. "It doesn't feel uncomfortable or sad. Not at all. Perhaps because I'm completely changed. As a ghost, my old life is so unavailable to me that I can't even miss it." She pauses and I'm sure her foot is still drawing circles. "Mostly, I feel grateful. Grateful that your dad figured out a way to keep life good for you and Sam. Paula's been an amazing addition to the family. So, no, it's not sad."

Listening to my mom talk about this makes me realize how far away from being a grown-up I am. It would drive me crazy if Josh started dating someone else. Luckily, he's not interested in dating. He's just interested in hours and hours of water polo time.

"Do you think your dad is happy and content?" Mom asks.

I shrug. "I really don't know because we don't have these kinds of conversations. But based on the way he avoids talking about you, I bet he's not so cool with everything."

As my mother flies off and the smell of coffee gets fainter and fainter, a little idea begins to bud in my mind.

chapter
nineteen

Dad, Junie and I go out for pizza and then to the movies. I even manage to talk Dad into a little video arcade fun. Finally, when Junie and I are lying in bed, talking over our exciting day, I get a chance to fill her in on Leah.

The next morning, Junie and I laze around our hotel room in our jammies. Junie's reading the paper, which lands each morning in the hall outside our door. I'm watching YouTube on her laptop. My dad drops off breakfast stuff before leaving to visit another client. I could get used to this lifestyle.

"Sparkling Pool a little later?" I say, smearing cream cheese on half a bagel.

"How far away is it?" Junie asks, pulling out her phone.

I wish I had a fancy phone like hers, instead of the dinosaur relic I own. Junie can hook up to the Internet no matter where she is.

I root around in my purse for my notebook, then read the address to her.

Humming "You Disturb Me," a song by one of Nick's favorite bands, Junie thumb-taps the address into her phone. "We can walk there. It's only a few blocks away."

"We have to get out of here without Leah knowing," I say. "She'll be a hindrance in the detecting department, and I can't take a chance of not cracking this case before we head back to Phoenix."

"You know I won't be any help at avoiding her," Junie says. "I can't hear, see or smell her."

I sigh. Leah is my loose cannon.

We finish eating, watch a little TV, then head to the bathroom. Junie flips on the lights. I haul out the makeup.

"We better put on a truckload," I say. "Like some of everything I brought. Foundation, blush, eye shadow, eyeliner, mascara, concealer. And no skimping. The more the better."

"I agree. We gotta do what we gotta do to look sixteen." Junie sets her glasses on the counter. "Did you bring your eyelash curler by any chance?"

"I brought everything." I plug in my flat iron. "We better do our hair too." I dig through some packages in my cosmetics bag. "And apply fake nails."

When our transformation is complete, we could easily pass for sixteen. Maybe eighteen in dim light. Twenty in the pitch black.

Flipping my hair back, I prance in front of the mirror. "We look so grown up, our parents would have to check our birth certificates to verify our true ages."

"I don't know about that." Junie bats her curled and heavily mascaraed eyelashes. "But this is as good as it gets. Any more gunk on my eyelids and I won't be able to hold them open."

Careful not to smudge our makeup, we pull two layers of tank tops over our heads and complete our outfits with skirts and sandals. My flip-flops are more comfortable, but when you're going undercover, you have to sacrifice comfort for disguise. And my sandals have more heel, which easily adds a few months to my age.

"Too bad we don't have flashier jewelry," I say, brushing on a final layer of eye shadow just below Junie's eyebrows. Really, she needs major plucking, but Junie doesn't get the pain-for-beauty thing yet. Maybe next year.

Junie holds her phone at arm's length and clicks our picture. She forwards it to Brianna with a text:
`<2 awesome older chicks in la!>`

Brianna texts back: <jealous in phoenix>

Junie and I paste on tough sixteen-year-old scowls and whip our purses over our shoulders. Then, legs in sync and arms around each other, we sashay down the hall to the elevators.

"Hey, girlfriend," I drawl in older teen speak, "did you get an eyeful of that hottie?" Amber sprinkles "hottie" into her conversation the way I sprinkle salt onto my fries.

"AP classes are sooo old-school," Junie says.

I'm just congratulating us on our undercover talents when the scent of Lippy's Root Beer Gloss breezes by.

"Sherry!" Leah says. "I've been waiting for you!"

I fake–Hollywood smile, and feel a little crack in my foundation.

"Leah," I say to Junie out of the side of my thickly outlined and lipsticked mouth.

"Who's that girl?" Leah asks.

"My friend Junie. From home," I say. "She can't hear you, though."

"Where are you two going? Not detecting, right?" Leah says. "Because I'm your partner, remember? To help me get over Michael. You're my therapy. And we need a detective meeting where you bring me up to speed on the case."

We arrive at the front door.

"Or are you two trying to get into an R-rated movie? In which case, I don't want to be included. Movies totally depress me. Because I won't be in one ever again."

I fling open the door.

Junie sails through.

"Leah, I'll catch up with you later."

On the sidewalk, I wipe the sweat off my forehead with the back of my hand. "I feel so bad. Leah is überneedy, but I only have three more days to solve this mystery."

"Sherry, your life is out of control." Junie stares at her phone screen, getting her bearings. "It's this way." She grabs my arm.

It feels like more than a few blocks, especially in my chic sandals. We trudge uphill, pass a purple hotel, a few restaurants and a bike shop. We keep up the older teen speak, tossing around words like "varsity," "SAT scores" and "social networking."

Located next to a sushi restaurant, Sparkling Pool is the end store in a narrow strip mall. Outside the pool store, there's a tall box of Styrofoam noodles.

I pull open the door and a bell rings. Junie and I saunter in.

A man calls to us from the middle of the store where he's stacking containers of chlorine tablets. "What can I help you with, ladies?"

"Ladies!" Junie whispers out of the side of her mouth. "We went overboard with the makeup. We by-passed teen and went straight to grandma."

"We look perfect," I assure her. "Maybe seventeen instead of sixteen." We bump knuckles for luck.

"Just browsing," I say, walking past a display of floating candles toward the male voice.

Like the Whac-A-Mole game at our local video arcade, the man's head pops up from behind a row of white plastic tubs. A head with large ears and close-set eyes. It's Derek Rizzo, the manager!

"Check out the sale merchandise in the far back corner," Rizzo says. "I put a bunch of pool toys on red-tag special this morning."

"Uh, okay, thank you," I say, patting my purse like it's an expensive Gucci, not a Target knockoff. And while I'm taking a second to regroup and figure out how to move the conversation around to me interviewing him, Junie jumps in.

"You provide a pool cleaning and repair service as well as running this store, right?" she says in a lower, adult voice. Although she may be dipping a little too low, because she sounds like my dad.

"Correct." Rizzo points to the counter. "Take a business card."

"Does your company clean pools all over Los Angeles?" I ask.

"Depends where you are." He hoists up a few tubs to start a new top row. "Where do you live?"

"In the hugest, fanciest mansion right in the middle of Beverly Hills," I say.

"Beverly Hills is our bread and butter." Rizzo comes to the front of his chlorine display and rotates a couple of tubs so the label faces out. "We probably clean eighty percent of the pools there."

"Do you hire girls?" Junie says.

"Sure." He shrugs. "We hire anyone who can do the job."

"Our neighbors, Melanie Grace and Jocelyn Dixon, are really happy with their pool cleaners," I say, using the same victims' names we tried on Cameron Williams.

"They're our customers." Rizzo smiles. "José's route, I believe."

"José?" I slap my hand to my chest in fake surprise. "They told us their pool cleaners were Lorraine and Stef."

Rizzo shakes his head. "No Lorraine or Stef on our roster."

"Maybe I got their names wrong," I say. When planning this part of the investigation, Junie and I talked about how Lorraine and Stef could've given us fake names.

Rizzo pulls a rag from his back pocket and begins

dusting the lids of the containers. "I don't have any females cleaning or repairing pools."

Junie frowns. "But you said you hire girls."

"I have a couple of girls who work in here"—he opens his arms and gestures around the store—"on the weekend. Selling, manning the register, that sort of thing."

Lorraine and Stef, or whatever their names are, could work in the store and get info for heists from a guy out in the field, cleaning pools.

"I thought you were looking for a pool service." Rizzo squints his too-close eyes at us. "If you're looking for jobs, don't bother filling out an application for me. I'll tell you right up front I don't hire anyone under eighteen. With my clientele, I need mature staff."

Junie thanks him quickly for his time, then gets behind me and practically pushes me out the door.

"What's the rush?" I ask her when we get to the sidewalk. "I wanted to check out the merchandise in the back corner. You know how I love to shop the sales."

She counts off on her fingers. "We could use something to drink. I'm ready for some R and R. You don't have a pool."

"All true," I admit.

Junie snaps oversized sunglasses on top of her glasses, then takes off speed-walking to the hotel.

She doesn't say a word the whole way back, just walks faster and faster, her arms out like a chicken's wings. When Junie is hungry or thirsty or tired, there's no talking to her. Of the two of us, I'm the easygoing friend.

We hit our room to change into bikinis, then it's down to the shimmering aqua pool. The blue sky is cloudless, with a white shining sun. A light breeze keeps the temperature perfect.

The pool area is crowded, but Junie snags the last two chaise longues. We're next to a couple with tattoos up and down their arms. On the other side, there's a mother and a little girl playing Go Fish. While Junie lays out towels, I skip over to the tiki drink station and order us tropical juices in coconut-shaped cups with bendy straws and mini umbrellas.

I'm slathering Junie's back with sunscreen carefully, because with her redheaded-freckly complexion, she burns faster than you can say "SPF 50."

"Lorraine and Stef have nothing to do with the pool company." Junie's lying on her stomach and her voice is muffled. "Well, at least not directly. I suppose they could be connected to an employee."

"Whatever way you slice it, we have no leads." I slouch. "Sure, we know the lengths Lorraine and Stef went to for the tickets. From your photos, we know they ripped off the purse. We know they're involved in the celebrity break-ins because Lorraine's bracelet is stolen property." I crunch an ice cube. "We know Detective Garcia is totally on the wrong track with both her suspects. Cameron Williams was at Dave and Buster's the night of the *Hollywood Girl* dinner."

Junie flips over and fishes her copy of *Rebecca* from her beach bag. "Well, we don't know why a few Beverly Hills residents thought he looked familiar."

I try to snap my fingers, but they're too slippery with leftover sunscreen. "At some point, we need to visit Taco Magnifico. See if we can rule out Cameron Williams for sure. After that, we're in a bind." I frown. "How are we supposed to find Lorraine and Stef in a ginormous city like Los Angeles?"

"Ginormous is right." Junie opens her book. "L.A. has a population of over ten million."

"I'm all tangled up in this mystery. I have no idea how to proceed." I bury my head in my hands. "And I can't even talk to my mom for ideas."

Junie's phone pings with a text.

I sit up.

She reads it, then taps back a reply. The twinkle in her eyes tells me it's Nick.

To anyone passing by, we look like a couple of best friends catching a few rays together by the pool of an upscale Hollywood hotel. But really, we're on different planets. Junie's on the Planet of Nick. I'm on the Planet of the Beverly Hills Bandits.

Junie's texting back and forth with Nick. Nonstop.

I get up and walk into the dim lobby. I flop on a cool leather chair and close my eyes. Maybe a little time alone will clear my mind. Like the letter cubes in a game of Boggle, I'm shaking up all the facts of the case, flipping them over, bumping them against each other, hoping for some patterns.

Then I smell it.

And my stomach drops.

chapter
twenty

"**S**herry!" Leah squeals. "When did you get back? I've been waiting for you. Did you look for me? I was hanging out at 25 Degrees. I thought you'd check there since that's where we first met."

Underneath her excited high pitch, I sense Leah's feelings are hurt that I'm not all best friends forever and wanting to hang with her every second.

And it suddenly hits me how überlonely she must be. What if our situations were reversed and I was a ghost while my mother was still alive? What if I'd been stuck in a hotel, no matter how fancy-pants, for a whole year after a nasty breakup, with no friends and no family to vent to?

"I have an idea," I say. "Let's try getting you outside."

"Seriously?" Leah barely breathes out the question.

"I don't know how my mother learned to cross thresholds. It was part of her classes at the Academy of Spirits." I open my beach bag. "But I'm wondering what would happen if I just walked out with you."

There's a quick breeze, then my beach bag gives a shake.

I pull the drawstrings tight, and stand. I square my shoulders and march to the door that leads to the pool. Who knows what's in store for us. But I'm hitting it straight on.

I step through. My bag shudders. And keeps on shuddering. I gather it against my chest. The shuddering slows, then stops. I untie the drawstrings. "Are you okay?" I ask softly.

"I feel kinda sick." A root beer scent wafts by my head. "But look! We made it!" The scent swirls and whirls. "A tree! A flower! Dirt!"

I'm meandering around the deck, heading toward Junie. Every few steps, Leah squeals about something. "How did I live a whole year without all this? Sherry, you are so the best!"

Junie's still texting. She'll probably end up with thumb blisters. I drop into my chaise longue and stretch out. Reaching under the chair, I retrieve my drink and take a long sip.

"I feel brand-new," Leah says.

"Cool beans," I say.

"What?" Junie looks up from her phone screen. She finally notices there's a whole world out here that doesn't revolve around Nick and a little screen and even littler keys.

"Leah," I say.

She nods and goes back to her phone.

"Got any fives?" the young girl near me asks her mom.

Apparently, this is the Go Fish game that never ends.

"She does," Leah whispers, even though no one can hear her but me. "That kid's totally owning her mom." She pauses, and I'm sure she's watching the card game intently. "Sherry, I rocked at Go Fish when I was a kid."

"Me too." I turn to Junie. "Not sure if you've thought of this, but you're messing with your tan line by hunching over your phone so much. Your face is still as white as Wonder Bread, while your arms and legs are freckling up."

"Whatever," she says, head still bowed.

"I smuggled Leah out of the hotel. In my beach bag."

Junie looks up. "Very smart!"

"Not all friends would think to help out in the

tan-line area," Leah says. "I don't think Junie appreciates you."

"She appreciates me," I say. "When she's not texting her boyfriend."

"Remember, I can't hear her," Junie says. "But I *can* hear you."

I hop up. "I gotta walk around. You know how sometimes your legs go all twitchy, and it's tough to sit still? Well, that's what my whole body and my brain's doing." I start pacing.

The root beer gloss scent trails along beside me. "I can really get into character. It's one of my strengths as an actress," Leah says.

I hold my cell against my ear to give myself a legitimate reason for talking aloud.

"And while I was waiting for you, I devoted the day to getting into the character of a detective."

"Oh yeah?" I'll admit I'm less than enthusiastic. Leah is completely inexperienced. I don't want to be mean to her, but I also don't want her messing up my investigation.

"Did the break-ins occur during the day or at night?" she asks.

"Both," I say. "But more at night."

"How about this for a strategy? We'll hang around Beverly Hills every night and patrol the area. Because now we know you can get me out of the hotel." Leah's talking faster and faster. "I can fly up and down the streets while you walk them. I'll be the Beverly Hills Security Ghost. You'll be the Beverly Hills Security Teen. We'll catch the thief red-handed."

"Leah, I'm not pounding the Beverly Hills pavement all night long. First off, my dad wouldn't let me. Second, I'd be exhausted, so I'd sleep all day. What's the point of coming to Los Angeles, then snoozing through the vacation? Third, I'd have blisters. Fourth, I doubt we'd catch someone. There isn't a break-in every evening." I've paced all the way around the pool and right out to the little tile fountain at the pool entrance.

Leah blows out a long breath. "You're absolutely right. I didn't take all that into consideration."

I sit down in a metal chair by the fountain.

"Here's another idea," Leah says. "It's common knowledge that criminals make mistakes when they're stressed. So, to stress the bad guy, or guys, take out an ad in the *Los Angeles Times*. A lot of people read that newspaper, even criminals. In the ad, say you know their identity and you're watching them, just waiting for them to trip up. And that you'll be ready with handcuffs."

I rub my forehead. She really is not helping. "Leah, I get less allowance than anyone else at my middle school. I could never afford an ad in the newspaper. Plus, it just wouldn't work."

I stand up and meander along a path around the

periphery of the hotel. It's pretty and Californian, with palm trees and benches and recycling bins. From the root beer smell, Leah is glued to my side.

Suddenly, I catch a whiff of coffee. I spin around. The smell is getting stronger. My mom is headed my way!

"Leah?" I stop and face where I'm pretty sure she's floating. "You know how parents can be difficult? They don't understand why you've got to do certain things?" I'm talking quickly, the words tripping all over each other. I've got to get through to Leah before my mom starts chatting with her, and Leah spills about the mystery. "And they'll be all over your case for next to nothing? And it's easier and actually kinder to them if you leave them in the dark about your activities? Because they can't worry about what they don't know?"

"What?" Leah asks.

"My mom! My mom is almost here! And she doesn't know I'm working on the mystery. And it's better if she doesn't know."

"Oh wow, I'll get to meet your mom! Just like real live girlfriends!"

"Did you hear me, Leah?" If I could, I'd grab her by the shoulders and shake her.

"I'm supposed to tell your mom all about how you're hunting down the Beverly Hills Bandits."

"No, no, no!"

"Psych!" Leah says. "I got it. Really. No mystery talk. My lips are sealed."

Phew. I think.

"So we're definitely working together, right?" she says. "And you're not going to avoid me anymore? And we'll hang out a bunch and be best friends?"

Leah's more on the ball than I realized.

"Hi, Sherry," my mom says.

"Mom," I say, "this is Leah."

"Pleased to meet you," my mom says.

"I'm very pleased to meet you too," Leah says. I can just imagine she's jumping up and down like a little kid. "Your daughter is amazing. And thoughtful and kind. Thanks to her I finally got out of this hotel today."

The two of them go on to discuss crossing thresholds, Leah's early death and other spiritual matters.

"Sherry told me you're trying to get to the bottom of Marilyn Monroe's death," Leah says. "Was it murder? Was it a suicide? Was it an accident?"

"Have you met her?" my mother asks.

"No, but about a month ago, I heard her calling over and over from the mirror she haunts, 'Joe DiMaggio, Joe DiMaggio.'" Leah's voice goes all breathy and squeaky.

"Interesting." I bet Mom's twirling a few strands of her dark hair around an index finger, a habit she has when she's mulling stuff over. "Rumor has it that she and DiMaggio, her second husband, were planning to remarry, but then she died."

"If I hear her again, I'll definitely tell Sherry so she can inform you," Leah says.

"Thank you." Mom and I make mother-daughter plans for tomorrow. She whispers how proud she is of me for befriending Leah. Then she takes off for a meeting with the Marilyn Monroe Spirit Sighting Club.

I continue my pacing.

"About the victims? Who are they?" Leah asks. "Is there any sort of pattern?"

I'll give her one thing. She's all over this mystery like a rash.

"Do you have a list or something I can see?" she says.

Why not? I have nothing to lose.

I hold open my beach bag, and a root beer gust whooshes in. The bag shivers as we cross back into the hotel. When the elevator arrives, I jump in. It's full of people, silent and staring at the buttons.

I pull my room key from the bag, and Leah zips out. Briefly, I press my finger against my lips. In an elevator, my goal is to quietly blend in.

"Maybe I'll notice something you haven't," Leah says by my ear. "You know, a fresh pair of eyes."

I give the slightest of nods.

"I'm a fountain of movie trivia. And I've picked up

even more this past year with all the premieres that take place at the Roosevelt."

Still radio silence from my end, but it's not computing with her.

"Like, for instance, Hannah Smyth won't go anywhere without a teacup dog in her pocket. Which sounds sort of cute. But even teacup dogs have to do their business. Guess where she stashes the miniature poop?"

I imitate the faces of those around me, glassy-eyed and frozen so that I look like a normal person who doesn't chat with the dead.

"In that gigantic potted plant by the front door. The staff can't figure out why it's dying."

"Seriously?" The word bursts out of my mouth before I can stop it.

Everyone in the elevator sidles away from me.

We hop out on the eighth floor, giggling. We giggle the whole way down the hall and into the room.

I boot up Junie's laptop, click straight to her photos and pull up the pictures of Detective Garcia's file. "Here's the list of celebrities whose homes were burglarized."

In like four seconds flat, as if she's a ghost speed-reader, Leah says, "Ha! That's not a mystery. That's a piece of cake."

chapter
twenty-one

"Leah," I say, "what are you talking about?"

"The victims? The celebrities whose homes were burglarized?" The papers on the desk flutter where Leah's swirling around. "They were all Raccoonites!"

"What's a Raccoonite?"

"The Raccoonites? From *After School with Uncle Stanley*?"

"Never heard of it."

"It was an after-school TV show. A kids' variety show."

I shake my head.

"You would've been too young for it," Leah says. "You were more *Sesame Street* back when it was on."

"We're basically the same age. You were more *Sesame Street* too."

"My big sister was a Raccoonite. I was the baby sister who tagged along. The invisible kid who hung around, but was never included."

And now she's the invisible ghost who hangs around. My heart goes tight. "Who were the Raccoonites?"

"Kids roughly nine to thirteen. They sang, danced, did dumb magic tricks. They'd introduce cartoons. And act out these little situations with morals at the end. Some of the Raccoonites went on to become big names, like the people on this list."

"Who's your sister?"

"Jocelyn Dixon."

"How did Detective Garcia miss this pattern?" I ask.

"Well, the show's been off the air for ten years or so," Leah says. "Plus, it's a little bit complicated." I can practically hear her puffing out her chest with pride. "For example, my sister totally changed her name when our mom remarried. As a Raccoonite, Jocelyn was Lyn Jones. Hannah Smyth changed her name from Melissa Smyth. Melanie Grace used to be teeny tiny, but look how tall she is now."

"Where does Dear Elle fit in?"

"She was a Raccoonite for like two minutes. Sherry, she was so bad. She couldn't sing or dance or act. She could barely breathe right. But her dad was a bigwig at the station. Anyway, she's completely reinvented.

Cosmetic surgery like crazy. And, of course, she used to have a last name. Funkleburger. Eleanor Funkleburger."

"Wow, Leah. You're incredible!"

"Thanks! And you were right. This totally beats moping around over Michael." She giggles. "Aka Sox Throck."

"How come the celebrities themselves aren't seeing the pattern?" I ask. "Wouldn't they remember the other Raccoonites?"

"But it's not like they're all still friends or anything," Leah says. "And there were many Raccoonites."

"I bet the victims don't know the names of everyone whose homes have been broken into," I say, thinking aloud.

"I wonder who'll be next?" Leah says. "Maybe Kira Cornish. She's one of the biggest stars that came out of that show."

"Why would someone go after the Raccoonites like this?" I say. "Jealousy? Someone who never achieved fame?"

"That describes a lot of Raccoonites," Leah says.

"Maybe it's someone who hated *After School with Uncle Stanley* and wants to seriously annoy everyone who did well because of the show," I say.

"Or someone who hates forest animals," Leah suggests.

Sometimes that ghost does not even make sense. "I want to pay a visit to Taco Magnifico. See if I can figure out why Cameron Williams looked familiar to a couple of Beverly Hills residents," I say. "You up for it?"

"Am I up for it? Are you kidding me?" Leah says. "I've been stuck in this hotel for over a year. Even a trip to the Dumpster sounds exciting."

I call down to the front desk and read off the restaurant's address from my notebook.

"It's just around the corner," the girl says. "Stop by the concierge, and he'll point you in the right direction."

I phone Junie. "You will not believe what Leah just figured out." And I tell her about the Raccoonites stuff and how Kira Cornish might be next and why it was easy for Detective Garcia to not see the connection.

"That's incredible," Junie says.

"We're walking to Taco Magnifico now. Just to see if there's something there to explain why those Beverly Hills people recognized Cameron Williams."

"Are you okay going without me?" Junie asks. "'Cause I'd like to even out my tan some more. But I can work on it later if you need me."

"I'm totally good," I say.

Leah and I head down to the lobby, where she flies

into my purse before I step out the door. The purse doesn't shudder as much as the beach bag did. Maybe we're getting the hang of this threshold-crossing thing.

I stride right into Taco Magnifico before unzipping my purse.

The second she's out, Leah starts complaining. "I'm cramping up in your micro purse. Any chance of upgrading?"

"Sorry about that," I say. "But, uh, no. My last purse was a huge black hole, swallowing up all my stuff."

Taco Magnifico is like a million other taco restaurants across the Southwest. A TV blares out a Spanish soap opera; the menu hangs on the wall; you place your order at a ceramic-tiled counter; the eating area has about ten little tables and chairs; and your mouth majorly waters.

"Don't look now," Leah says, "but the guy sitting at the first table is checking you out."

Of course, now all I want to do is look.

"Uh-oh. He stopped fiddling with the salsa bottle. He's standing up. He's walking toward us."

"How old? How cute? Just getting a soda refill?" I say.

"Are you staying at the Roosevelt?" It's the dark-haired, dark-eyed guy from the hotel gift shop.

"I am," I say. "You?"

"Ask him if he's available," Leah says. "A rebound boyfriend wouldn't be a bad thing for you right now."

"Me too." He glances around the restaurant. "You eaten here before?"

"No. This is the first time I've set foot in the place." I point to the menu. "I'm getting a fish taco. It's sort of my test dish for all Mexican restaurants."

"Mine too!" he says. "If I don't like the fish taco, I'm outta there, and I won't be back."

"That's exactly my theory!" I say.

"Moving the conversation right along," Leah says. "'Hello, Cute Boy from Hotel, do you have a girl-friend?'"

Leah and I are definitely having a chat about ghost etiquette when we get back to the hotel.

"The Mexican place directly across from the hotel? Next to the tattoo place?" I press my thumb and index finger together. "Awesome fish tacos."

"Thanks for the tip," he says. "I'm Mark, by the way. Mark Peña." Everything about him is smiley and friendly, from his chocolate eyes to his warm voice.

"I'm Sherry Baldwin."

"Are you here on your own, Sherry?"

I look around like I might actually find Leah. "I'm with a girlfriend. She's kind of weird, though. Always disappearing."

"Hey," Leah says. "That's not nice."

170

"So, Mark, I was just wondering"—I stick a quarter in the vending machine, all nonchalant—"do you play water polo?"

"No, I'm more of a land-sports kind of guy," Mark says. "Why?"

"Just curious." I turn the knob and a handful of Mike and Ikes tumble out. I offer him some.

"Get his cell," Leah shouts.

"Thanks." He takes a couple of candies.

"Mark, your order's ready," calls the girl behind the counter.

"That's me," he says. "We didn't realize they delivered. My parents are waiting for me back at the hotel." He looks right into my eyes. "See you around?"

"Sure."

Mark grabs his order and gives me a final wave as he shoulders open the door.

Leah's right in my ear. "Are you crazy? Why didn't you get his number? Do you not want to move on from Josh?"

But what's echoing in my mind is a little sentence Mark said: We didn't realize they delivered.

chapter
twenty-two

Back at the hotel, I find Junie in our room. Along with a huge basket of fruit and candy.

"It's for you," Junie says. "*Hollywood Girl* had it delivered."

"Wow," I say. "What if this was actually our life?" I gesture around at the fancy room and the basket.

"It'd be pretty cool," Junie says. "But we might miss Arizona after a while."

"You're probably right." I hand her a brown paper bag.

"Fish taco?" That's how well Junie knows me.

I tell her about Mark Peña.

"Does it feel weird"—she looks up from opening

her cardboard food box—"to be interested in someone who's not Josh?"

"Yeah. My heart is so confused." I dip a chip in
salsa. "It's like our first day at Saguaro Middle
School. When we didn't know where any of the
classes were, and we were in a daze, trying to find
our way around." I nibble the edges of the chip.
"That's what it's like for my heart."

Junie squeezes lime on her taco. "Sounds tough."

"Anyway, guess what's interesting about Taco Magnifico?" I don't wait for a reply because Junie's mouth
is full of food. "They deliver. To Beverly Hills. I talked
to the manager, and Cameron Williams does some of
the deliveries. So that easily explains how he looks
familiar to a few of those Beverly Hills residents."

"Any chance he's scoping out their homes while
he's on delivery duty?" Junie says.

"I don't think so. Not unless we can come up with
a way to link him to the Raccoonites." I poke shred-
ded cabbage back into my taco from where it fell out
into the box. "Can I use your computer?"

While I'm waiting for the laptop to boot up, I bite
into my taco. "Not up to my standards."

"You're so picky," Junie says. "I'll eat yours if you
don't want it"

I Google Kira Cornish. "Junie, Kira Cornish is a
humongous fan of Pink's hot-dog stand. It's the place

173

she's most spotted by the paparazzi. She even has a hot dog named after her."

"And?" Junie says.

"The other day, Lorraine and Stef showed up here out of the blue. Just hoping to meet me," I say. "Maybe they'll do something similar to Kira Cornish. Basically hang out at Pink's and wait to see if she makes an appearance."

"And then would they talk to her?" Junie munches on my taco. "Ask her what she has worth stealing?"

I shrug. "It's a long shot. But it's all I have right now. Plus, I'm hungry. Are you coming?"

"I ate my taco and part of yours. I'll go with you just for the detecting part, though," Junie says. "Although, you shouldn't have a hot dog either. You know what's in them, right?"

I plug my ears. Some mysteries are better left unsolved.

Junie stands. "I feel so gross after lying outside. I'm taking a shower before I go anywhere."

"I'll text my dad about Pink's," I say. "We already talked about going together."

I pull out my phone and tap in a message.

`<im starving 4 a hot dog. Pink's hot dog stand for lunch?>`

Then I sit down at the desk with nail polish for a touch-up. My dad's the slowest texter in the West. I'm unscrewing the cap when my phone pings with his reply. Junie hasn't even found her shampoo and conditioner yet.

`<yes!!! Be in the parking lot in 15.>`

He must be starving. He's never texted that fast in his life. I'll do my nails later. I read the text to Junie.

"Just go with your dad," she says. "I can veg here. You guys could use some time together."

I head to the hotel parking lot and am reclining in one of the leather couches by valet parking, when Dad slowly noses in and stops by the curb. At the speed of a bicycle, we drive to La Brea and Melrose.

"Sherry, this is one of your best ideas," Dad says, glancing over his shoulder for the fifth time before changing lanes. "I haven't had a hot dog in months."

Not since he married The Ruler and her health-food ways. He turns right into Pink's, and we leave the car with valet parking. Yes, valet parking at a hot-dog stand!

We join the ordering line on the sidewalk. I keep an eye peeled for limos.

"Let's eat inside," I say. "Follow me." I balance my tray with a Grape Crush and a twelve-inch Kira Cornish dog, which comes with relish, chopped tomatoes and bacon.

I find a table for two next to the wall. We're seated by rows of signed black-and-white photos of celebrities who have eaten at Pink's. It's like eating lunch while a bunch of celebrities stare at you. Of course, Kira Cornish's photo is up.

Across from me, Dad's eyeing his order and rubbing his hands. His dogs are coated in bright orange nacho cheese, lumpy chili and sauerkraut. His onion rings glisten with grease. His bottle of Strawberry Crush sweats blobs of moisture. His grin couldn't be wider.

Dad takes a bite, then wipes his chin. He swallows. "This is the best hot dog I've had in my life. And that's saying a lot." Dad picks up an onion ring and waves it at me. "Feel free to help me eat these." Closing his eyes, he chomps down. "Did I ever tell you about the time I won a hot-dog-eating contest at summer camp?"

"Yeah. And you were sick and throwing up for two days after, right?" I point at his tray of fat and cholesterol.

"What?" He follows my finger. "Don't worry. This is nothing your old man can't handle."

"Are you going to try to beat Orson Welles's record?" I nibble at my dog. Überyum.

"Orson Welles? What record?"

"For the most dogs eaten in one sitting at Pink's. Eighteen!"

"I don't think so. That's over my limit." Dad laughs. "How do you know that odd little fact?"

"Mom," I say simply.

And that word, "Mom," hangs like a curtain between us. She doesn't come up much in our conversations. Certainly not nearly as much as I'd like her to. I want to hear the old stories over and over so that Sam and I don't forget them. Stories like the year I pulled down the Christmas tree, or when I cut Sam's hair, or when Sam cooked the plastic play food in my Easy-Bake Oven.

But the word "Mom" sends my dad's eyes flitting back and forth.

At least, usually it does. But today, he nods. "Your mother had a head full of Hollywood trivia, didn't she?"

"Yeah, she was like a walking encyclopedia of it."

"Remember the year she threw an Oscar party and everyone came dressed up?" Dad says. "Then, before the ceremony started, she handed out ballots so we could vote on all the categories."

"There was a piece of red carpet running down the walkway to our front door." I have this very vague memory.

"It was a great party," Dad says. "And your mom was the star of it."

"Grandpa played his accordion and sang songs in German, right? And Grandma danced me through the house?"

"That's the way it happened." He smiles.

The two of us sit in silence, eating and drinking in the warm glow of a connection.

Dad breaks the cozy silence. "So, uh, how're you feeling about things with Josh?"

At a different time and in a different place, I'd shut him down at this point. What teen girl talks to her dad about a broken heart? But today is special. Maybe because it's the two of us and we just tripped down memory lane about Mom. Plus we're far from home and we're indulging in a meal only we would eat. The feeling of awkwardness between us is gone.

"I'm sad. It hurts. Then sometimes I forget about how Josh and I are broken up. Then I'll see something that reminds me of him and it's like getting knocked over by a bus. Onto a road of spikes."

"That's heartache," Dad says. "I don't have any advice. But I can tell you time heals."

"Is that how it is for you with Mom?"

He sets his hot dog down. "Sherry, I will always love your mother. Always. I still miss her. I avoid eating at Tio Roberto's because it makes me feel bad. But even with all the memories of your mom, I can love Paula too."

"If you could talk to Mom, is there anything you'd tell her?" I ask.

Dad stares into the distance. "There are lots of things I'd like to tell her. I'd bring her up-to-date on

178

you kids. How well you're both doing." He coughs. "I'd like her to know how much our life together meant to me. How I still take her opinions into consideration when I'm making decisions for you and Sam." He swallows. "I hope she'd be happy with the way I've handled things since her death."

A huge lump sits in my throat. "I'm sure she'd be happy with you, Dad." I think back to the idea I had at Grauman's Chinese Theatre when my mom was asking about my dad. My parents would so benefit from five minutes of Real Time. Five minutes where they could talk face to face.

There's a strained silence. Dad forces a laugh. "Love is a strange business. No doubt about it."

"I hear you," I say.

"Sherry, you're really a terrific person. A wonderful daughter. A great big sister."

I roll my eyes.

"I'm not just saying this because you're my daughter." Dad picks up an onion ring. "I liked Josh. Thought he was a nice kid. But he's obviously an idiot. And there will be plenty of other boys." He frowns. "Way in the future. Maybe wait ten or twenty years."

I shake my head and smile.

"Hey, did I tell you the joke I heard the other night about the traveling accountant?"

He did, but I let him tell it again.

"You okay for a minute, Dad? I want to ask the staff a few questions. For Junie's article."

"Definitely." He waves me away from the table. "This place should be featured in the school paper. How many hot-dog stands are around for over seven decades? And cater to both the stars and the riffraff."

I walk up to the cashier. There's a lull in business, and he's free to talk.

"I was hoping to bump into Kira Cornish," I say. "Does she come here pretty often?"

"Maybe once a month," he says. "Did she have a new movie release? Two other girls asked me about her earlier today."

The hairs on my arms jump to attention. "Did one girl have an eyebrow bar and the other a nose ring?"

"Haven't got a clue," he says.

The girl behind him who's filling up the fridge with bottles of soda says, "Troy, seriously? Do you go through life with your eyes shut? Yes, they did. They practically looked like twins. They both had brown hair, and it was the exact same length. To their chins."

Troy shrugs. "I don't remember any of that."

The girl sighs. "Do you remember that you told them to go on the tour of the stars' homes if they want to catch sight of Kira Cornish's awesome digs?"

chapter
twenty-three

My dad's upstairs in his room, lying down and sipping on Alka-Seltzer.

Junie, my mom and I are at the concierge's desk.

"Three—I mean, two—tickets for a tour of the stars' homes," I say. This tour was so meant to be. My mother had already suggested the tour for the three of us. And now I'm hoping it'll help me figure out what Lorraine and Stef are plotting.

"Air-conditioned van or open-top minibus?" the concierge asks.

"Whichever one goes past Kira Cornish's house," I say.

"Kira Cornish?" my mom says. "Since when did you become a fan of hers?"

"Very recently," I say.

"Pardon?" the concierge says, alternately staring at me and his computer screen.

"We're interested in seeing Kira Cornish's house," Junie says.

"Only one company's allowed up that particular street. Starline, the company that runs the open-top van." The concierge's fingers fly across his computer keyboard. "Let's see if they have seats available. The van only holds ten. And they pick up from other hotels too."

"How come other tour buses can't go on that street?" I ask.

"The residents complained. The other companies weren't strict enough, and there were incidents involving trespassing and cameras with zoom."

"How disrespectful," my mom says.

"Got it!" the concierge says. "These are the last two tickets."

Junie and I unzip our purses and pull out money.

"You'll be glad you chose this tour, even though the ride's a little rougher." He sticks his hand out by the printer to grab our tickets. "Vista Drive ends at the top of a hill with a great panoramic view. You can get out, look around. Just stay away from private property. We don't want Starline to lose their privileges too."

We shove the tickets in our pocket and tramp out to the parking lot to wait.

When the minibus arrives, I give the passengers a once-over. No Lorraine or Stef.

We bump along over to Beverly Hills, the sun beating down on our heads. I'm queasy from the exhaust of the other vehicles on the road. Junie and I have to scream to hear each other over the street noise and the minibus's growling engine.

"I'm hot," Junie says. "Are freckles popping out all over my face?"

"No." I grab my roiling stomach.

"The breeze is beautiful," Mom says.

The driver keeps up a running monologue. We pass two-story houses and one-story houses, houses with arches, palm trees, wide leafy trees, lots of green lawns and fancy cars. He slows down and even stops so we can snap lots of photos. With his microphone, he calls out homeowners' names and tidbits of information, like movies they've been in or how long they've lived in the house and the names of previous occupants.

All very interesting if you're in a comfortable ride with air-conditioning.

"I'm gonna suggest they überdiscount this tour to make up for the discomfort," I say. "I'll be lucky if I don't throw up."

"I'll be lucky if I don't turn into a beet." Junie's shielding her face with her notebook.

"I can't wait to see Jane Russell's house," my mom says. "She and Marilyn Monroe were friends."

We're chugging higher and higher up a steep hill. The driver pulls over to the side and idles whenever a vehicle appears behind us. "Sorry, folks. I know this slows down the tour. But the residents have been getting vocal, and we're the last company still allowed in this neighborhood." We lurch the rest of the way up.

I'm hanging over the side, clutching my stomach.

Junie's crouching down to avoid the rays.

At the top, the driver parks, then stands and faces us, his back against the dashboard. "On the right we have Kira Cornish's humble abode." He opens his arms wide. "On the left is Jane Russell's house. Jane Russell costarred with Marilyn Monroe in *Gentlemen Prefer Blondes*. Ms. Russell has a second house in the Central Valley, and spends most of her time there."

"I wouldn't be at all surprised if Marilyn Monroe hangs out here. Think of the peace and quiet," my mom says, all perky. Obviously the harrowing, stinky, jerky ride has been no hardship for her.

The nanosecond the driver opens the side door, I bolt out, gasping for fresh air and stable ground.

Junie is close on my heels. "I'm not feeling so good either," she moans.

"Remember, folks, you're free to take photos of the homes and the view," the driver says. "But no playing amateur paparazzi. Absolutely no trespassing."

"The 'no trespassing' rule does not apply to me." My mom giggles like she's our age again and at a slumber party. "Fingers crossed, girls, that there's a sign of Marilyn Monroe here." The scent of coffee briefly hovers above me, then wafts away.

"No littering." The driver continues on with his list of rules. "We don't want to lose access to this hilltop."

"What a horrible tour." Junie stumbles behind me. "I won't be recommending it in the school paper."

When we get to the grass, she slumps down, sitting cross-legged, and wipes the sweat off her forehead with the back of her hand. "I feel like my brains are going to explode."

The other passengers step around us. They're oohing and ahhing about the view. They frown at us like we're poor sports.

I take a deep breath. "Actually, Junie, now that I'm off that death trap of a minibus, I'm feeling a little better." I stretch out my arms and legs. "Although my thighs are still tingling unpleasantly from the vibrating seats."

"Go scout out the place. Take some photos with your phone of Kira Cornish's house." The hair around

Junie's face is damp and wispy. "I'm not moving." She closes her eyes. "Don't do anything dumb, Sherry."

I don't even dignify that with a response. I'm a detective. A professional detective, except for the getting paid part. At this moment, though, I'm a detective without a real plan.

I meander over to Kira Cornish's one-story stucco house and stand at the foot of the driveway. A black wrought-iron fence surrounds the property.

I glance over my shoulder. The guide and the rest of the tour group are across the wide street at Jane Russell's house. He's yakking away, his arms gesticulating like a windmill.

I walk to the side of Kira Cornish's house. I'm standing on rubble, completely still, staring at the house, at the low hedge snaking around to the back.

A pudgy brown bunny hops past me, then stops and balances on his haunches, his nose twitching. He scampers off, disappears from my view, then seconds later is in front of me but on the other side of the fence. I follow his trail. The fence curves around the property, then suddenly ends. I could walk right into Kira Cornish's backyard.

If I were crazy enough to ignore the warnings from the concierge and the bus driver and even Junie. Which I'm not.

I take a step closer to the last post.

Nothing's moving. Not even a leaf or a blade of grass. Then the bunny bounces down an embankment in the backyard.

And out of sight.

In the distance, I can hear the tour guide's voice. "Folks, see all the agapanthus at the front of Kira Cornish's house? Those are Kira's favorite flowers. Word has it that these were transplanted from her mother's garden down in San Diego."

From below the embankment, there's a squeal. "Stef, look, isn't that the cutest bunny in the world?"

chapter
twenty-four

Lorraine and Stef are out of sight, at the bottom of the embankment in Kira Cornish's backyard!

The tourists and tour guide are still at the front of the house and out of sight.

Junie is back near the bus and out of sight.

My heart is in my throat.

I make a split-second decision.

Fast as a speeding comet, I streak around the end of the fence. I leap down the embankment. Yikes. It's steeper than I expected. *Thud.* I trip. I roll. *Thud.* I come to a halt by a pair of flip-flops. Hollywood High flip-flops.

The bunny bolts.

Lying on my back, I look up and wave. "Hi, Lorraine!" I shield my eyes with my other hand. "Hi, Stef!" This situation is going to take all the pluck I can muster.

I stand slowly, checking for broken bones. Then I brush off the dirt. "Thought I'd find you two here."

Their jaws hang open.

"How'd you find us?" Stef finally gets her mouth back in gear.

"A little clue here, a little clue there," I answer. I smile, all friendly and best friends. I pretend like the whole use-me-for-tickets-to-pull-off-a-purse-heist thing never happened.

"I can see how you won the essay contest," Lorraine says. "You really are smart."

"I am," I say. "And you know what else I am?"

"A gymnast?" Lorraine says, pointing at the hill.

Exercising great self-control, I don't roll my eyes. "No, a celebrity hound."

There's a crunching-gravel sound from above as the tour group, minus Junie and me, tromps along the side of the house.

"Folks, here is Kira Cornish's wishing well. Any pennies you throw in, she promises to donate to an animal shelter." He pauses. "Five more minutes of enjoying this beautiful area, then it's back on the minibus for a few more homes." The driver's voice comes from straight above me. "Okay, people, I'm going to insist you return to the street. We can't risk losing the privilege of bringing our tours up here."

The tour group's voices fade.

"We can't risk losing the privilege, blah blah blah," Lorraine mimics. "He sounds just like the last tour guide. They must memorize a script."

"Were you on the last tour?" I ask. "Is that how you guys got here?"

"No way. Too expensive." Lorraine's wearing about five ankle bracelets. They tinkle when she moves. "We just got the address of this house from them."

"How'd you know Kira Cornish isn't home?"

"This guy we know said she's filming in Toronto," Lorraine says.

"How'd you get up here?" I ask.

"Same guy." Lorraine pulls her hair back in a ponytail, then lets it drop. "He has a driver's—"

"You were really looking for us?" Stef interrupts.

"Absolutely," I say.

Stef crosses her arms. "Why?"

"Because of this sweet thing you have going," I say.

Lorraine's eyes are blurry with confusion. Stef hugs her elbows tighter till the points are like white embers.

"The Beverly Hills Bandits." I smile at each of them in turn. "It's you and you."

Lorraine's jaw goes slack again. This is not an attractive look for her.

Stef's whole face wrinkles in a frown. Very prune-like.

And while they're still in speechless shock, I add, "Talk about a brilliant scheme. Breaking into celebrities' homes, stealing things you can sell for money and giving yourselves a chance to nab some cool personal stuff too." I sigh. "And the way you stole Dear Elle's purse? Totally amazing."

"Sherry's incredible," Lorraine says to Stef. "She's probably part genius."

"Thank you," I say. "That means a lot."

Stef watches me through narrowed eyes.

"We really have picked up some cool stuff, Sherry." Lorraine pulls on the hem of her T-shirt. "This is Melanie Grace's." She twists her wrist, which jiggles the bracelet with the dog charm. "Hannah Smyth's."

"You know what I never figured out?" I say. "How did you guys know I had extra tickets for the *Hollywood Girl* bash?"

"We didn't," Lorraine says. "We knew there'd be security, and we thought you'd let us walk in with you. We had no idea the security would be so crazy tight. We just got lucky that you gave us the tickets."

"What do you want from us?" Stef says.

"I want in," I say.

chapter
twenty-five

"Seriously? You want to break into houses with us?" Lorraine says. "You ever done anything like that before?"

"No, but I gotta start somewhere," I say. "And you guys seem like you'd be good teachers."

Stef is looking skeptical to the max.

"I love anything and everything to do with celebrities," I say. "I started watching the Academy Awards when I still had a pacifier in my mouth." I place a hand over my heart. "To take home stuff owned by a star would be the best souvenir ever."

"Let's take her to tomorrow's meeting," Lorraine says.

"Please," I wheedle. Tomorrow's meeting?

Stef purses her lips.

"Plus, David wants us to find a new girl for the next job," Lorraine says.

David? I decide now is not the best time to ask questions. I remain quiet and put on my sad, cute puppy-dog look. It always works with my dad.

"When do you go back to Phoenix?" Stef asks.

"In three days," I say, hoping this will be enough time.

Stef turns to Lorraine. "We can't just show up at the meeting with her. Not without checking with David first."

"Stef's right," Lorraine says to me. "David's kind of moody. You don't want to make him mad." She shakes her head like she's clearing out a bad memory.

"I'm free tomorrow." My voice rings with enthusiasm. "All day."

"Sherry. Sherry." Junie's weak voice comes from the top of the embankment. "Where are you?"

"Is that your wimpy friend?" Lorraine asks.

"Wimpy? More like brainy." The words shoot out of my mouth quickly and reflexively. Defending Junie might not be the brightest thing I can do in terms of this case. But that's the way it is with best friends; you can't let anyone dog them.

"Sherry, everyone from the tour is looking for you," Junie calls softly.

"Can you check with David?" I ask.

193

"Stef, you could call him," Lorraine says.

Stef scowls. "Fine. What's your cell?"

I give it to her quickly and she punches the number into her phone.

"We're asking about *you*," Lorraine says. "Not your friend. Don't even tell her what's going on."

"Sherry Baldwin!" booms the tour guide's voice. "Report immediately to the minibus!"

Yikes!

"Get out of here!" Stef says. "Before you get us caught!"

"Sherry Baldwin! Sherry Baldwin!" calls a choir of voices.

I scramble up the hill.

Race to the end of the fence.

I almost make it undetected.

Almost.

I have one foot on Kira Cornish's property and one foot off, when the tour guide and a line of his henchmen tourists round the corner of the house.

Their eyes zero in on me.

Junie limps behind them, sunburned and a palm pressed against her forehead.

The driver points a long arm in my direction. "You. To. The. Bus. Now."

When we reach the vehicle, he says, "Sit up front. By me."

My mom flutters in and settles on the window side

194

of my seat. "Sherry, what's going on? Did you and Junie have an argument?"

I give a slight shake of my head.

The driver shoves the vehicle into gear and starts in on me. "What were you thinking? How much plainer did I need to make it? No trespassing. You and your entire family are banned forever from Starline Tours."

As soon as my mom figures out why I'm in trouble, she starts in on me too.

For the entire ride, my left ear is bombarded by the tour guide and my right ear is bombarded by my mother. Except for Junie, all the passengers are shooting me hate stares.

Finally, we arrive at the Roosevelt. Ears burning, I escape from the bus.

Junie follows me to 25 Degrees, where we collapse in a booth and order a pitcher of soda.

"So, why'd you do it?" Junie says. "Why did you trespass?"

While I'm texting my dad to let him know we're back, I say to her, "Before I tell you, answer this: Do I look different?"

She gazes at my face. "Yes, you do."

"I knew it." Some paths you choose in life mark you. Not like a big black smudge. More like a light bruise that doesn't even show in all lights. But it's there. You don't feel it happening, but you're changed forever. I just chose a very scary, very illegal path. "Hardened? Mature? Overwrought?"

Junie frowns. "You're sunburned across the nose, and there's dirt on your chin."

With the back of my hand, I wipe my chin. "Not superficial stuff like that. I'm talking deep, character-building changes." I pause dramatically. "Junie, I'm infiltrating the Beverly Hills Bandits."

"What?"

I fill her in. "So, if all goes according to plan, I'll be at tomorrow's meeting with the thieves. And I'll be in on the next heist."

"How did I miss it? You do look different." Junie leans across the table and grabs my shoulders. "Your eyes are totally crazed. Your left pupil's dilated more than the right one. Did you fall on your head? Hard?" She drops my shoulders. "You're out of your mind!

"You think your mom and Mrs. Howard are mad at you now? Wait'll they find out you're going illegal and hooking up with a burglary ring to solve a mystery they told you to ignore. The World Wide Web for the Dead will go wild with this." Junie's shaking her head so fast, it's fuzzy and fat, like I'm looking at her in a mirror at the fair's haunted house.

"Junie, chill." I make a time-out sign with my hands. "I have not lost my mind. I'm not really a thief. I went undercover to get information about the next operation," I say slowly, to make sure she understands, and there's no reason for this big freak-out. "Next, I'm going to spill all to Detective Garcia. Together, we'll catch David and the bandits in action."

"Sherry, you watch too many crime shows. Just hand everything over to the detective. Before you are *t-o-a-s-t*."

I'm about to explain patiently that I'm seeing this case through to the very end, when our booth fills with the scent of Lippy's Root Beer Gloss.

"Sherry!" Leah squeals. "I've been looking everywhere for you. Where have you been?"

"It's Leah," I say to Junie. "Long story," I say to Leah.

"The longer the better," Leah says. "I'm so bored."

Junie stands. "I'm going to take some random photos around the hotel." She looks at me long and hard. "Think about what I said, Sherry."

Shoulders straight, Junie strides out. She's so sure of herself, so sure her way is the best way to wrap up this mystery. I sigh. Junie is a scholar and a mathematician and a potential astronaut. She is not a detective.

"What's her problem?" Leah asks. "She's the draggiest friend."

"No, no, she's a good friend. We just don't see eye to eye on this thing." Every time I turn around today, I'm defending Junie. Because that's the kind of good friend I am.

"What thing?" Leah asks.

I tip the pitcher, topping up my glass. Then I fill her in.

"You're joining a burglary ring?" Leah squeals. "You are so brave. No wonder you don't miss Josh. You stay so busy. And your life is so exciting."

"I *might* be joining a burglary ring. Depends if I get invited to tomorrow's meeting."

"Oh, you will. They so want you."

Leah's much easier to listen to than Junie. Even with her squealy pitch and overuse of the word "so."

"I want to be just like you," Leah says.

Definitely easier to listen to.

"Sherry, I just made a decision. I'm coming to the meeting."

"No!" It's like someone punched me in the gut. "This is one of those situations I need to handle on my own."

"Absolutely not," Leah says. "We're partners. No way I'm letting you go into such a scary, dangerous situation on your own."

"I might not even be going."

"Oh no, you're going," Leah says. "You're so persuasive. Look how you even talked me out of my depression. My *yearlong* depression."

Obviously, I'll be sneaking out of the hotel. I'm not taking Leah. No ifs, ands or buts.

My cell phone pings with a text.

"Is it Lorraine and Stef?" Leah asks. "With details about tomorrow? I knew they'd want you in. You need to trust my judgment more, partner."

That ghost is überenthusiastic about everything. Hard to believe she was a depressed head case just a few short days ago.

"It's Brianna," I say. "A friend back in Phoenix."

"Another friend?" Leah asks sharply, a little jealousy tingeing her words. "How many friends do you have?"

"You'd like Brianna," I say. "She's crazy in a good way. Boy crazy, makeup crazy, clothes crazy."

"Uh-huh," Leah says, not sounding convinced. "She sounds a little out of control."

I click on Messages.

> `<im @ the phoenix mall. Josh`
> `is here!!!! Following him>`

I go oatmeal mushy inside. "Brianna's at the mall. She spotted Josh, and she's following him! Josh and I have so many memories at the mall. I bet he's super down and visiting all our old places, thinking about me."

"You guys are so getting back together," Leah says.

> I type. `<where exactly r u?>`
> `<couple of stores bhind him.`
> `Hes approaching video world>`
> Brianna replies.

I catch a strong whiff of Lippy's Root Beer Gloss as Leah hovers by my shoulder. "Did you two play a lot of video games together?"

"Tons. We almost entered a competition at Video World as a team," I say. "I bet his heart is heavy with memories right now."

```
<josh passed video world. Didnt
even slow down>
```
Brianna texts.

"Probably the memories are too severe," Leah says. "He can't bear to even set foot in the place."

```
<josh approaching naked
makeup kiosk>
```

"Now, this will be very painful for him," I say. "I solved a mystery where someone was sabotaging the makeup at that booth. And Josh helped. Walking by that kiosk must be like an arrow stabbing his heart."

"Makes sense to me," Leah says.

```
<josh smiled & waved 2 amber>
```

"He's a really nice guy. Probably he doesn't want to burden Amber with his pain." But the oatmeal mush inside me is starting to bubble.

"I bet he's working hard to hold back the tears," Leah says.

> <josh turning in2 food court.
> Passing american potato
> company. Walking 2 middle
> where tables & chairs r>

"It almost sounds as though he's meeting some-one," Leah says. "I mean, who goes to the food court and doesn't buy food? Unless it's a meeting place. Does he have a buddy who works at the mall?"

I shake my head slowly.

> <OH NO!!!!> Brianna screams
> through her text.
> <WAT???> I text.
> <Sherry, take deep breath. Josh
> talking to hi skool girl. They
> r leaving food court 2gether>
> <is she ugly?> I text.
> <no. ubercute>
> <how do u no shes in hi skool?>
> <wearing hi skool t-shirt.
> Looks older than us>
> <hi skool t-shirt? So, she
> has zero fashion sense?>

```
<shes wearing gorgeous denim
skirt ur saving up 4>
```

The oatmeal mush is boiling up a storm in my stomach.

"Maybe they're cousins," Leah says.

"I've met all his cousins," I say.

"She could be a long-lost cousin. They could've connected through Facebook," Leah says. "Ask if they're holding hands. No one holds hands with their cousin."

```
<r they holding hands?> My
```
whole body tenses.
```
<no . . . >
<wat does all the . . . mean?>
<she keeps bumping up against
him. Hip 2 hip. Laughing>
<wats his facial expression?>
<idk. Im bhind them>
<where r they now?> I ask.
<OH NO!!!>
<WAT???>
<theyre holding hands>
```

"Ask if their arms are swinging," Leah says. "Or if they're doing the static handhold, where their arms are basically hanging because they don't really like each other and don't really want to hold hands, but feel like they have to."

I type in the question, crossing my fingers that the reply will have the word "static" in it.

```
<swinging like monkeys>
```

I think I'm going to be sick.

```
<OH NO!!!>
<wat now?> How much worse can it get?
<shes leading him into jazzd
up juice>
```

"Jazzed-Up Juice? Never heard of it," Leah says. "Sounds very unromantic. Sounds like the kind of place you take your long-lost Facebook cousin who forced you to hold hands with her."

"It's 'our' place. Mine and Josh's. We shared enough smoothies there to last a lifetime," I say in a choked-up, on-the-verge-of-tears voice. "We had 'our' table and 'our' plastic chairs in the corner. Jazzed-Up Juice is romantic with a capital *R* for me."

"Turn off your cell," Leah says. "This is like sticking a curling iron in your eye."

```
<want to no wat theyre
talking about?> Brianna asks.
```

"No, you do not," Leah says firmly. "Tell her to go shopping."

```
<Sara says josh is staring
nonstop at hi skool grl, so we
can easily get table near them>
<Sara? We?>
<me, Sara, Margo>
```

Brianna, Sara and Margo? That trio is the opposite of subtle and quiet. Those girls are more along the lines of obvious and giggly. I lay my weary head on my arms. Josh is sharing a romantic smoothie with a sophisticated high school girl in an expensive skirt while his eighth-grader ex-girlfriend's friends are trailing after him through the mall. Acting like Disney Channel detectives.

I text Brianna.

```
<Do NOT follow them into
jazzd up juice. Go away>
<id forgotten how cute he is.
I don't know why u ever let
him go>
```

Leah turns off my cell.
This is the worst vacation of my life.

chapter
twenty-six

Dad, Junie and I exit the hotel and saunter down Hollywood Boulevard to number 6667. It's the home of Musso and Frank Grill.

"Musso and Frank is Hollywood's first restaurant," Junie says. "It's been around since 1919."

Junie's knowledge of trivia often gets on my nerves. But this evening, her voice nattering on about the unimportant soothes me. Like lotion on raw skin.

"Lots of famous people used to eat here. Such as the writers Ernest Hemingway and F. Scott Fitzgerald," Junie continues. "Even now, movie stars come to this restaurant."

My dad is still a little pale from his hot-dog

overindulgence. He hasn't told a joke, good or bad, for hours.

"You okay?" I ask him.

"*Comme ci, comme ça.* I'll live." It's Céline's influence.

"*Il ne faut pas nous accompagner,*" Junie spouts off.

"*Pardon,*" my dad says in a bad French accent.

"Enough." I am not filled with patience right now. First, my mom and the bus driver were all over me about stepping on Kira Cornish's property. Then, I learn that Josh is seeing an older girl and my love life is a train wreck.

"You don't have to come with us," Junie says.

"I needed to get out of that hotel room," my dad says. "Especially with those walls the color of hot-dog buns. Bad memories."

He opens the door to the restaurant, and we take a major step back in time. It reminds me of the restaurants you see in old Hollywood movies. The lighting is dim. The furniture is dark and heavy. The tables are covered with white tablecloths. It's comforting, like mashed potatoes.

A short maitre d' glides over to us. "Table for three?" he asks in a hushed tone.

He leads us to a corner booth. The seats are dark red leather. I open my long menu.

"Sherry, guess what I see?" Junie says in a singsong

voice, like I'm two years old and she's trying to convince me to eat my smushed peas. "They have ravioli."

She's aware of my love of ravioli and is trying to be really nice. Back at the room, we had a long powwow about the texts from Brianna. Junie promised to talk to Nick about Josh, to see if Nick has any idea what's going on. But the bottom line is, Josh is moving on. It doesn't matter what Nick knows or doesn't know.

My dad orders a chef's salad with dressing on the side.

"Smart thinking, Dad," I say. "Take it easy on the old stomach."

"That tasty, unhealthy rich food." Dad smacks his lips. "It was good while it lasted."

I end up going for the ravioli and dare Junie to try a tongue sandwich.

Of course, Dad sticks out his tongue and wiggles it around. This passes for humor in my family.

"Yuck." Junie grimaces and chooses the chicken sandwich.

We're kicking back, waiting for our food, when Dad's cell phone rings. It's The Ruler. They chat for a few minutes about what's going on at home and the touristy things we've done here.

"Paula wants to tell you hi." Dad passes me his phone.

"How are you doing, Sherry?" she asks.

My chest goes tight. Strangely, I want to confide in her about Brianna and the mall and Josh. But I'm scared I'll lose it. And that would be majorly awkward in a public place, like a restaurant. "I'm okay." I swallow. "Basically."

"You've been on my mind," she says. "This is such a tough time for you."

For a math and computer teacher, The Ruler can be amazingly perceptive.

"It is," I choke out.

My dad's focused on a roll, intent on spreading the butter thin and evenly and tuned out of the conversation.

Junie's watching me carefully.

"Sam and I will definitely be ready to have you home. The house is too quiet without you and your dad."

We talk a little more about how Grandma is recuperating nicely. Then The Ruler switches topics. "Your fish are exhibiting some strange behavior. They swim fast at each other, crash and sometimes bump each other into the side of the aquarium."

I close my eyes. They have never done anything like this before. And I'm not even close by to be able to calm them down.

"Do you want me to call the pet store?" The Ruler asks.

"Sure," I say. But with the way my life is going, I don't think there's much point.

I'm poking my fork into a steaming bowl of ravioli when my phone pings.

Junie watches me even more carefully while I snap open my cell to read the text. I only hope it isn't Brianna.

It's from Stef. `<11 oclock.`
`Tomorrow. Central library.`
`Teen room>`

chapter
twenty-seven

After a late breakfast the next morning, my dad drives off to see a client. Junie and I sneak through the hotel. I poke my nose around each corner, sniffing for a clear coast. There's a brief moment when I think I catch a whiff of root beer, but then it's gone. Phew. We manage to avoid Leah and make it out onto the street. This burglary-ring meeting will be tricky enough without keeping track of a ghost tasting a little freedom.

Junie hitches her laptop bag over her shoulder, and we head to the Metro, where we buy tickets for the Red Line to the Pershing Square station. We disembark and walk along West Fifth to the Los Angeles Central Library.

And the teen burglary-ring meeting.

The Los Angeles Central Library is tall and echoey.

"Look at the incredible architecture," Junie says. "This would make a fascinating article for the school paper."

"Not so much," I say. Admittedly, I'm on edge with the upcoming rendezvous. But I haven't lost my common sense.

"Are you seeing what I'm seeing?" Junie says. "The painted ceiling, the chandeliers, the lanterns. It's amazing."

I roll my eyes.

We ride the escalator up to Teen 'Scape, the teen area.

"Amazing," Junie repeats. "The elevator ride alone is worth a trip here."

At Teen 'Scape, I peer through the glass, waving Junie behind me. Lorraine and Stef didn't want her to even *know* about the meeting. They probably don't want her anywhere near the library.

"Are they there?" Junie asks. "How many of them are in the group?"

"It looks like a big video-game challenge." I squint. "Lots of kids, with controllers, sprawled on beanbag chairs." A hand to my forehead, I cover up against the glare. "I don't see Lorraine or Stef anywhere."

The door opens. A librarian, her badge swinging around her neck, pokes out her head. "Come on in, girls. We're starting up a new game of *Alien Invaders* in a few minutes."

"Alien Invaders!" I say. "I rock at that." So does Josh. But I am so not going there. I'm at a huge library in L.A., seconds away from going undercover, if I can find the gang. I push Josh out of my mind. Which is exactly what he did to me.

"You'll be up against some stiff competition." The librarian smiles.

"Actually, I'm meeting people, but I don't see them," I say.

"Oh, you're the new book club member." The librarian claps. "What did you think of *Fahrenheit Four Fifty-One*?"

Fahrenheit Four Fifty-What? It sounds like a science textbook. I open my mouth. "Well—"

"Censorship is such a timely theme," Junie jumps in.

Censorship? That doesn't sound very scientific.

"I agree." The librarian flutters her hands with excitement. "And the way Granger referred to mankind rising up again like a phoenix? I like that message."

The librarian and Junie are nodding like a couple of best-friend bobbleheads.

"The book club?" I prompt.

"Of course!" The librarian gazes at Junie like she's the next shining star of the club. "You too?"

Junie shakes her head.

"The video challenge?" The librarian's shoulders slump.

"Definitely not," Junie says.

"We have to do what we can to get them into the library," the librarian says apologetically.

"Come find me when you're done, Sherry." Junie slaps her laptop bag. "I'll be working on the school newspaper."

"For free wireless, you'll want the computer center in the Bradley Wing on lower level three." The librarian pats Junie's back. "You've made my day, dear. You have no idea."

This is the kind of effect Junie has on grown-ups. Arizona. California. Probably worldwide.

I follow the librarian past the gamers to a small seminar room. She taps on the closed door, then cracks it and sticks in her head. "I found your newest member." She steps to the side, presses a couple of fingers into the small of my back and gently pushes me forward.

"Hi, Sherry," Lorraine says in a subdued voice.

Stef gives me the smallest of waves.

Another teen girl, with purple-streaked long hair, is sitting on her hands and staring at a blank wall. Blue and pink heart tattoos dance up and down her arms. She doesn't even acknowledge me.

The air is thick and tense and sticky with electricity.

A balloon would automatically cling to the wall without me rubbing it on my head. Just entering the room, my mouth dries up with nerves. I unzip my purse to pull a hard candy from my emergency stash.

The scent of root beer fills the room. Leah!

I freeze, my eyes round like I'm at a horror movie.

"I darted into your purse when you were racing down the hall. With all the running, your purse was banging against your leg, so you probably didn't notice the shaking this time. I think I felt a little less nauseated," Leah says. "By the way, Sherry, partners look after each other. They don't sneak off and leave one behind. You might want to remember that."

I breathe in slowly. I lower my eyes, trying to compose myself. Leah could ruin everything. Everything. I have to block her out. Smell no Leah. Hear no Leah. Speak to no Leah.

At the head of the table is a guy. He's all casual and leaning back in his chair, one leg crossed over the other. In a white Hard Rock Cafe Hollywood T-shirt and faded blue jeans, he looks marginally older than Amber, maybe nineteen.

"He's the bad guy?" Leah whistles. "Who knew a bad guy could be so adorable."

My lips are squeezed shut.

"Thanks, Mrs. Patron." The guy beams at the

librarian. "We can get going on the book in earnest now."

She closes the door and leaves me standing in this charged, but silent, room. The kind of silence before a big storm.

"I'm David." The guy pins me with his gaze, and it's like the other girls magically vanish, and the small room is empty except for David and me. Grinning, he runs a hand through his messy hair. He's somehow cute and cool and geeky all at the same time. His teeth are straight and sparkly, and a dimple dots his left cheek.

"So, you're Sherry Holmes Baldwin, talented detective and writer of essays about true love."

"Yeah," I say.

"One essay," Leah says. "You only wrote one essay on true love."

He uncrosses his leg, pushes back his chair and stands. David's taller and thinner than I was expecting. Walking around the table and over to me, he bounces on his Nikes, like a little boy excited to make a new friend.

David looks the opposite of a bad guy. Except for his eyes. They're as cold as the ice dispensed by our fridge door.

He extends a hand. "I've been looking forward to meeting you."

We shake; then he gestures to the seated girls. "Of course, you already know Lorraine and Stef." He inclines his head at the third girl. "This is Taylor."

"Hi, Taylor," I say.

Taylor does a half-nod thing and the metallic purple streaks in her long hair shimmer. I've met friendlier people.

"It's like they're all zombies or something," Leah says. "Does he scare them into acting like that?"

"So, what did Lorraine and Stef tell you about me?" David asks.

"You pick houses with good stuff. And you always know when the owner is gone." I don't mention the moodiness.

David pulls back a chair. "Have a seat, Sherry."

He returns to his place at the head of the table. I'm across from Lorraine and Stef. Taylor is at the end opposite from David. I can smell Leah right next to me. At least I'm the only person who can smell the root beer and knows she's here. I want to tell her to get lost, but I can't risk even a whisper. I have to look normal, together, reliable—like a thief you want on your team.

"Why is it you want to get involved with our operation?" David asks.

I turn so that I'm on an angle, facing him. I realize that this is a sort of job interview. He's not letting me in just on the strength of Lorraine and Stef's suggestion. I swallow a couple of times to get rid of the cotton-ball feeling in my mouth. "I'm crazy for everything Hollywood." I continue with the script Junie and I worked out on the train ride from the hotel to the library, injecting perkiness and enthusiasm into my voice.

"Good answer." Leah claps.

David's tapping his fingers against each other. His eyes bore into me like I'm an interesting specimen he found in his garden. "And you'd do anything to get your hands on celebrity belongings?"

"No, not anything." I blow out a breath. There are some things I just can't lie about and still sound sincere. "What you guys are doing, yes, I can handle that, easy schmeasy. But, no, I wouldn't do just anything. Like, nothing violent."

"An honest thief!" He slaps the table. "That's not something you see every day, is it, girls?"

"He likes you," Leah says. "You are so getting this job."

"No, David," Lorraine, Stef and Taylor say, all monotone.

David smiles and the dimple dents his cheek again. "Tell me a little bit about detecting. What's the secret to figuring out a mystery?"

I gulp. Junie and I did not plan for this question. I'm quiet for a second, gathering my thoughts. The strategy for acing this interview is to be up-front when possible, I think. "There isn't a big secret. You just have to keep working it. Like you know how when you first dump a jigsaw puzzle out of its box, there's a thousand or whatever pieces and you can't even imagine how you're going to connect them all up. But you just get a little method going, like starting with the corners, and you keep poking away at it. Every time you walk past the puzzle, you try a couple of pieces. And, eventually, you're done and you're getting out that special glue to hold it all together."

"You didn't mention having a brilliant partner," Leah says.

"In your opinion," David says, "are the police close to finishing the jigsaw puzzle of the Beverly Hills Bandits?"

"Nope." At least, not until they get my help.

David winks at me. "'Cause I'm too smart for them." He reaches under the table and hoists up a denim backpack. From it, he pulls out a few loose dry-erase markers and an eraser. He goes to the whiteboard propped up in the corner and draws a road, a house, a shed and a fence that suddenly comes to an end. Kira Cornish's house!

"Lorraine and Stef did an excellent job scoping out the site of our next operation."

"Thanks," Lorraine and Stef say in unison.

Taylor scowls.

"The artwork is in the shed at the back of the property." David marks a red *X* on the shed on his map. "The door has a flimsy lock." He draws a happy face on the shed door. "Lorraine and Stef saw a ton of electronics through the windows on the bottom floor of the house." He sketches an old-fashioned TV with an antenna. "We'll get a huge haul. Lorraine, Stef and Taylor, you'll be working hard. But you'll have time to rip off some souvenirs. Doesn't Kira Cornish collect little glass animals?"

"What about me?" A flutter of panic takes flight in my chest.

With a few quick strokes, David places a stick-figure person walking a stick-figure dog on the road in front of Kira Cornish's house. "This neighborhood doesn't like strangers. You were on the tour, right? So you know they're only allowing one bus company up there. A girl walking a dog doesn't raise any red flags. You could be Kira Cornish's little cousin. You even look young for your age."

I let the insult slide.

"I agree," Leah says. "You could pass for ten."

"When a curious neighbor comes out—and at least one will—you tell them you and your mom are house-sitting for Kira, and your mom noticed the automatic cleaner wasn't working in the pool and called for a repair. You're walking the dog and watching for the repairman." David draws a van with a rectangle on the side. "I'll throw a magnetic pool-company sign up on my van."

"I'll keep you company," Leah says.

"So I'm just a lookout person," I say, secretly relieved.

"Your role is more critical than that," David says. "You head off trouble before it starts."

"I'll get you a glass animal, Sherry," Lorraine says. "What kind of stuff are you into? Dogs? Cats? Horses?"

I'm about to answer fish, particularly bala sharks. And then give her a brief description so she can tell them apart from any generic glass fish that Kira Cornish might have in her collection.

"Not now, Lorraine," David snaps, in a tone that basically calls her a moron.

Lorraine goes silent, blinking rapidly.

Like they're hypnotized, Stef and Taylor keep their eyes downcast.

"The heist will be tomorrow," David says. "Stef will text you when we're ready to roll."

Tomorrow? I'll have to ditch Leah and get Detective Garcia on board pronto.

Taylor clears her throat. "Why her? Why does she get to be lookout?"

"Sherry looks naive, innocent, boring. Not like the three of you," David says. "See any piercings on her? Any brassy hair streaks? Any tattoos?"

Naive? Innocent? BORING?

Humming, David erases the whiteboard, then drops the eraser and markers into his backpack.

Then he straightens up and—*fwap!* He whacks the table hard. An inch from Taylor's elbow.

I jump.

The other girls jump too.

Leah squeals.

"What did you mess up at the last house?" David barks at Taylor.

"The key," she mumbles.

"Speak up," David says, "so everyone can hear. Especially our newest addition."

"Forgot to bring you a key," Taylor says a little louder. Her eyes glisten.

Detective Garcia was right about the key souvenir.

"Is it that difficult to grab a key? Any key?" David stands too close to Taylor, towering over her. "Lorraine and Stef managed to steal a purse in a crowded room. And guess what was in the purse?"

"A key," Taylor whispers.

"I don't like putting you girls in dicey situations like the *Hollywood Girl* event. But I had to, didn't I, Taylor? Because of you. Because you didn't pick up a key from that job." David crosses his arms. "You need to get with the program."

She cowers. "It won't happen again."

"It better not." David still doesn't step away from

her. "If it does, some other lucky moron from your pitiful high-school drama club will have your spot."

High-school drama club recruits. Stolen keys as souvenirs. The Beverly Hills Bandits strike again tomorrow.

And David is the scariest kind of bad guy.

Unpredictable.

chapter
twenty-eight

After David dismisses us, Taylor takes off like a flash. Lorraine, Stef and I traipse to the restroom together, because even burglary girls hit the restroom in groups.

I hang back and let them go in first to give me a few minutes in the hall with Leah. The nanosecond the door closes, I whisper, "Did you recognize David? Was he a Raccoonite?"

"He didn't look familiar to me," Leah says. "But that doesn't mean a whole lot. Maybe he had a bit part. Maybe he changed a bunch in the last decade. Maybe he never was a Raccoonite."

"Sherry," Lorraine calls through the shut door, "do you have a brush?"

I'm not supposed to loan out my brush or comb or hat or hair clips. The Ruler's orders. She has a huge phobia about lice. But in the interest of the case, I'm breaking the rule.

I scrounge around in my purse for my brush, then walk in and hand it to Lorraine. She, Stef and I preen in front of the mirror.

Leah hangs next to me, her Lippy's Root Beer Gloss scent right by my face.

I pop open my eye shadow container.

"That's a cute color. Is it raspberry? That's one thing I hate about being dead." Leah sighs. "I'm missing out on all the new makeup."

"It's pomegranate," I say.

"What?" Lorraine and Stef say.

Ack. I hold out my eye shadow. "Isn't this adorable? It's pomegranate." Obviously, I need to keep on ignoring Leah.

"Sure, I'll try it." Lorraine exchanges my brush for my eye shadow. That girl is big into borrowing.

"So, what's the deal with the drama club?" I ask.

"You haven't heard of the Hollywood High Players?" Lorraine is aghast.

"I'm from Phoenix." I unscrew my mascara tube. "Remember?"

"Sometimes I forget," Lorraine brushes thick streaks of pomegranate across her lids. "You seem pretty normal for someone who doesn't live in California."

That's so messed up. Everyone knows California is home to the nutcakes of the nation. I keep this wisdom to myself.

Stef clips on eyelash curlers. "My lashes are totally drooping today."

"Hollywood High's a magnet school for drama." Lorraine hands me my eye shadow. "David usually guest speaks to the theater kids a few times a year. That's how he found us."

"What does he talk about?" I pump the plastic wand up and down, coating it heavily in mascara. "Certainly not how to get along with people."

Lorraine laughs. Even Stef cracks a smile.

"He talks about acting." Sucking in her cheeks, Lorraine blends in blush. "When he was a kid he was on a TV show."

"Ask which show," Leah says.

"Really?" The hairs on my arms prick up like mini detective antennae. "Which show?"

"I know he told us. . . ." Lorraine shrugs. "There were a bunch of kids. They sang. They danced. It sounded lame, and, anyway, he was nothing special on it."

"Sounds like *After School with Uncle Stanley*," Leah says.

"What about after the show ended?" I ask. "Was he still on TV?"

Stef makes quotation marks in the air. "'David Hughes Peaks at Ten Years Old.'" She grins. "And it's been downhill since then."

Hughes? Now I have his last name. "Why does your high school want him as a guest speaker if he's a nobody?" I ask.

"People love him. He can be pretty chill when he wants to be. You saw that," Stef says. "And I think he does know junk about TV acting. He's had other TV gigs, just nothing major." Stef's wiping under her eyes where mascara has pooled. "I'm going to have to redo my eyes."

"Plus, our school likes him 'cause he donates a chunk of money." Lorraine wets a paper towel and hands it to Stef.

"Money he gets from the break-ins?" I say incredulously.

"Sure," Lorraine says.

"He's definitely not giving our drama club money he got from acting." Stef starts to laugh.

"Yeah, he could donate"—Lorraine chokes out—"a whole five cents. If it were from his acting."

The two girls are clutching their stomachs, doubled over with laughter.

"David's such a bully," Leah says, "it must feel good to make fun of him."

I give a slight nod while unscrewing the lid to my lip gloss. "How does he choose which houses to hit?"

"It's not like he confides in us." Stef hiccups, getting herself under control.

"Maybe based on how much expensive stuff they have?" Lorraine says. "And if the owner's gone?"

"What're the keys all about?" I ask, swiping on some gloss.

"He has one from every house we've robbed. He's really into that." Lorraine tips Stef's chin. "Try Sherry's eye shadow. The color's perfect for you."

I hand Stef my eye shadow. I'm shocked at how little Lorraine and Stef can answer about David. I'm even more shocked at how little they care about finding out. They are very go-with-the-flow girls. "You know what else I don't get?"

"You know what I don't get?" Stef says. "Why you're asking so many questions."

"She's right," Leah says. "Quit acting like a detective and just be a normal teen."

Linking arms, Lorraine and Stef take one giant step back from the mirror. United against me.

"Sorry. I'm trying to figure it all out," I babble. "Because he's such a jerk to you guys. I mean, do you really need him?"

"Do not wreck this for us, Sherry," Stef says, a steely glint in her eyes. "We want the celebrity stuff. David finds the best houses. Except for that one time with Dear Elle's house, nothing's ever gone wrong."

Even Lorraine morphs into a scary version of her former ditzy self. "Don't make me sorry I convinced Stef and David to bring you on." She juts her perfectly made-up face forward, frowning.

"Seriously, this is a sweet gig. So what if David's a jerk? We can handle it." Stef crosses her arms. "If you can't, get out now."

"Whoa," Leah says. "These girls are hard-core."

I put my hands up in the air, in a sign of surrender. "I can deal. I totally want the cool stuff too. Forget I even mentioned anything about David. I'm sure he could be worse."

I wait in the restroom after Lorraine and Stef leave.

"That was a close call," Leah says. "You almost got yourself kicked out before the first heist."

I splash water on my face. Leah's right.

"We gotta find out if he really was a Raccoonite," Leah says.

"I agree." I open the door and step into the hall. "I have an idea. Follow me."

Three thousand escalators later, I spot Junie at a table, hunched over her laptop. Earbuds in, she doesn't hear me coming.

I tap her shoulder.

She turns around with a jerk, removing a bud.

"Have you been here the whole time?" I ask.

"I got so much done." Her eyes are bright. "I can't wait to start posting articles." She pulls out the other earbud. "So, how did it go?"

I give her the scoop. "You gotta find information on this guy."

"Tell her I'm here too," Leah says.

"Leah wants you to know she's right next to me."

"Oh, yeah." Junie's already biting down on her tongue, which means she's in concentration mode. She's closing screens and pulling up search engines, typing fast.

"David Hughes," I say. "About twenty."

"Or nineteen," Leah chimes in.

"Make that nineteen or twenty," I say.

Junie is the queen of Internet research. If there's even a hint of a clue out there in cyberspace, Junie will scare it up.

The three of us are crowded around the computer screen.

"If he changed his name, I don't know how we'll ever find out about him," I say.

"Calm down," Junie says. "I've barely scratched the surface. Let me try going at this from a different angle." She loves a challenge.

"Maybe something's wrong with my theory," Leah says. "Maybe that's why Junie can't find a connection. Maybe it's not all about the Raccoonites."

Leah's sounding more and more like a real sleuth

229

with the way she questions herself and tries to find the theory that fits the mystery.

I relay Leah's concern to Junie.

Junie keeps typing. "Leah, can you tell me the names of some local communities around here?"

"Walnut Park, Glendale, Commerce," Leah tells me.

I add in a few more as Leah feeds them to me. "Oakwood, La Cienega Heights, Cahuenga Pass."

Junie's fingers fly over the keyboard. Images flash across the screen.

I sit quietly, twisting my hair around and around my index finger. Even Leah is silent.

And when it feels as though we're stuck in a big black nothingness of cyberspace where we're never moving forward and where we'll never find the answer, Junie snaps her fingers. "Bingo!"

Somehow, Junie manages to dig up the teeniest, tiniest online article about David Hughes and *After School with Uncle Stanley*. There's a head shot of David when he was ten. In some ways, he hasn't changed at all. He's got that cute dimple denting his left cheek. And he's wearing a huge Hollywood grin, which doesn't match his cold, unfriendly eyes.

The article quotes his mother as threatening to sue the variety show for not taking full advantage of David's extraordinary talents. Apparently, despite rehearsing a bunch with the Raccoonites, he only appeared briefly in one episode. His mother denies allegations of David bullying the other children in the show. She maintains he was ostracized.

Next, in her überdetailed way, Junie searches the names of all the victims. Leah provides the names that the actresses used as children. All the victims were members of the *After School with Uncle Stanley* cast around the time of the article. Including Kira Cornish.

"So, the actors whose homes were broken into were all on *After School with Uncle Stanley* at the same time as David Hughes?" I say. "Back then, he didn't fit in. And he really doesn't fit in now because they're all rich and famous."

"That pretty much sums it up," Leah says.

"Would they ever hang out with him now?" Junie asks.

"Are you kidding me?" Leah squeals. "They are so out of his league. Plus, he's creepy."

I repeat all this for Junie. Minus the squeal.

"Wow, I'm incredible," Leah says. "I aced my first mystery! Talk about natural talent. How many mysteries have you solved, Sherry? Ever solve one faster than me? I don't think so. Because I'm a natural. I'm the fastest."

Nothing worse than a gloating ghost.

"Sherry, let's get going." Junie logs off and pushes back her chair. "We don't have much time."

chapter
twenty-nine

Leah wants to fly along next to me, but I explain we need to try that when time isn't so of the essence. "Leah," I say, "a gust of wind could pick you up and blow you to Kansas. Who knows how you'll do as a ghost in the big real world?"

"I'm not saying I don't trust you, Sherry," she says, "but don't leave me locked up in your purse. It's small and dark and there's a smell."

After zipping her in, I sling the bag over my shoulder, and Junie and I trot off toward the Metro.

We find seats at the back of the train. Across from us, a young guy sits on the dirty floor, engaged in an argument with someone in his head. This is so not Phoenix.

Junie yanks her notebook and a pen from her back-pack and writes, *How exactly are we going to ditch Leah?* She passes me the paper and pen.

I don't know, I scribble back. *Now she's had some freedom and wants to hang with us all the time.*

Hang with YOU. Junie presses hard on the YOU, and the letters are thick.

'Cause I can talk to her. Please tell me my best friend isn't jealous of a ghost.

Junie takes the notebook and pretty much writes an essay. *It's going to be tough enough convincing Detective Garcia that she needs to jump on board and take over the case the way we see it. But if Leah's with us, you're half paying attention to her. Then you're listening to her comments and trying not to answer. Basically, you end up looking like a flake.* She shakes her head and adds another line. *We can't take Leah to the Beverly Hills PD.* Junie pauses, her pen poised above the page. *Tell her we're going for food.*

Me? Looking like a flake? I'm not even going there. *I think we should tell her the truth. We owe her that much.* I hitch my purse up higher. *She's been a huge help in this case.*

"Humph." Junie shrugs.

"Junie," I say, "you've been my best friend for forever." I point to my purse. "Not coming between us," I say. "But it doesn't hurt to be nice." I write

233

sideways on the notebook, which is on Junie's lap. *She's lonely. She lives miles from us. She's out of our lives after this trip.*

Junie nods slowly.

I look around. No one's paying one drop of attention to us. No one's wondering why two girls sitting side by side are passing notes back and forth. People are hooked up to earbuds or Bluetooths or the voices in their head. We're in a group, but at the same time, we're not. We're in a compartment with lots of other commuters, but we're also in our own private world.

Same thing with David and his teen gang. With a few copies of *Fahrenheit 451* as camouflage, they're meeting in a busy public library to plan burglaries.

In Los Angeles, they hide the secret stuff right out in the open.

The train pulls into Hollywood Station. We exit and head to the hotel.

"I'm going to grab some snacks from our stash in the room," Junie says. "I'll meet you back here."

"Grab the sour Gummis," I say, unzipping my purse.

A root beer scent rushes out. "Any chance you could invest in a backpack? Something a little roomier? And some air freshener," Leah says. "And please turn down your phone. A text came in and about gave me a heart attack."

"Leah, I am so not carrying a backpack everywhere I go." I pull out my phone. There's a text from my dad, checking in with us. "But I'll change my phone to vibrate next time." I text Dad back.

"Okay." Leah claps, ready for action. "What's next?"

"The Beverly Hills PD," I say.

She squeals. "This is too exciting! A chance to meet up with real detectives!" She pauses. "Not that you're not a real detective, Sherry. But at this point in my sleuthing career, I'm ready to deal with professionals."

"Actually, Junie and I are going to speak to the detective on the case by ourselves."

"What? You can't do that! You wouldn't be this far along without my insider knowledge!"

"Too true. You've been amazing, Leah," I say. "But you can't exactly talk to the detective. 'Cause you've got that whole ghost thing going, right?"

"I know I'm a ghost. I'm not a moron," Leah snaps. "Obviously, you'll talk for me. Tell the detective that I'm right there next to you. He can ask me anything, and you'll pass on my answers."

I put my hand up like a stop sign. "Leah, we need this detective to totally believe in our whole theory. Not to decide I'm some kind of, uh, flake from Phoenix who, uh, chats with ghosts. I'm sorry, but you have to stay here."

The elevator doors open, and Junie's walking over to me, a plastic grocery bag of treats clutched in her hand. "Let's go."

"Just give me a sec," I say.

"Oh, I get it," Leah says. "Now that I've shared my Hollywood knowledge, it's all about you and Junie stealing the glory."

"Is she still here?" Junie asks.

"What's that supposed to mean?" Leah says. "Tell her I'm still here because this is where I live. You guys are the visitors."

I stick my fingers in my ears and close my eyes. I count to ten, taking slow, even breaths. I open my eyes, grab the bag from Junie, then march to the door.

"What're you doing, Sherry?" Junie says sharply.

"Yeah, what's going on?" Leah asks.

I push on the door. "You two are stressing me out." I step into a yellow patch of bright sunlight. "I'm going by myself."

Luckily, I'm in Hollywood where dreams come true and where directors make sure everyone follows the script and events fall into place just as they should.

A checkered taxicab pulls up to the curb.

I hop in.

chapter
thirty

Last time, Dad and Junie came with me to the Beverly Hills Police Department. This time, I'm tackling it on my own. I walk up the cement ramp to the turquoise-trimmed double doors. With each step, I'm mulling over my strategy, figuring out how to talk Detective Garcia over to our side.

I pull open the door and cross the threshold. Behind the counter and protected by bulletproof glass, Officer Mullins messes with papers in a wire basket. Very déjà vu.

I'm starting to understand why the police haven't solved this case. They're caught in a time warp, never moving forward, just going through the motions.

"What can I do for you?" Officer Mullins roots

around under the counter. "I think we might have some—"

"I'm not looking for a coloring book," I say. "Remember me? I was here a few days ago, talking with Detective Garcia about the Beverly Hills Bandits?"

Officer Mullins scratches his head. "A lot of people find their way through our doors. I can't be expected to recognize all the faces."

"I need to speak with Detective Garcia," I say, skipping straight to the point. "I know where the next heist will take place."

The officer opens a little door in the glass and pushes through a yellow pad of paper and a pencil.

Not the pad-of-paper-and-the-pencil routine again. I refuse to be stuck in his time warp.

I grab my stomach and fake-groan. "Oh, oh, oh."

"What's wrong?" the officer asks, still pushing his writing materials through the glass. He's very one-track-minded.

"I'm gonna hurl all over the place." I paste a grimace of agony on my face. "Why did I eat that last really fat and greasy burrito? Why did I pour on a whole bucket of bright red, chunky salsa?" I punctuate my sentence with a belch.

"Stop!" Officer Mullins bangs on the glass. "Stop in the name of the law!" He pounds some more. "Do not throw up on the floor." More pounding. "Throw up in that bag you're holding."

I rattle the bag in the air. "This bag? It has candy in it. So, uh, ixnay on throwing up in it." I clamp a hand over my mouth and groan and moan. My acting has improved by leaps and bounds since my arrival in Los Angeles. Must be something in the air.

"I order you to open that bag!" Officer Mullins shouts. He's all pressed up against the glass, his big stomach flopped on the counter.

Instead of following orders, I dash to the stairs. I slide my hand from my mouth to my chin and call over my shoulder, "I'm a sprinter at sports day for my school. I'll make it to the restroom."

"Use the restroom on this floor," he calls out.

I fake-drag myself up the stairs, clawing the turquoise banister. I turn and burp loudly a couple of times. "Too nauseated to descend."

Officer Mullins sits down, safe behind his bullet-proof, vomit-proof glass.

At the top of the stairs and out of the officer's sight, I straighten. Then I'm off, dashing around the corner and down the hall to the Detective Division, where yet another officer sits behind glass. He blinks at me. "Yes?"

"Sherry Baldwin for Detective Tatiana Garcia," I say.

"She expecting you?"

"She sure should be," I say. "Please tell her Sherry's

239

here with information about which star's home will be broken into next."

He picks up the phone and mumbles away.

Within seconds, the door swings open.

"Hi, Sherry." Several strands of flyaway hair have escaped from Detective Garcia's ponytail. She looks like a mad scientist.

I'm barely seated when she starts quizzing me.

"Whose house do you think will be next?" she asks.

"Kira Cornish's. At the top of that big hill."

"Why?" she asks. "What are you basing this on?" She pulls a couple of Reese's Cups from her pocket and offers me one.

I shake my head and lift out the sour Gummi worms from the plastic bag. I pry off the lid, then tilt the container toward her.

She pulls out a green worm. What is it with detectives and sugar? It must help us think better so that we make connections and hook up the jigsaw pieces.

I talk about *After School with Uncle Stanley* and the actors' name changes and plastic surgery. Then I move on to the library meeting and Lorraine, Stef and Taylor. I describe David Hughes. I tell her about how he collects keys and how that explains the theft of Dear Elle's purse.

Detective Garcia's eyes never leave my face. I bet she doesn't even know she inhaled four peanut butter cups. "That's some amazing sleuthing work, Sherry."

"Thanks." I feel a little dishonest because I'm not giving any credit to Leah, but I really can't. Not if I want to remain credible.

"So, when are they planning the burglary?" Detective Garcia asks. "We'll set up surveillance and catch them in the act."

"Sometime tomorrow." I shrug. "Stef'll contact me to say they're on the way to pick me up."

"To pick you up?" Detective Garcia raises her voice. "You joined up with them?"

"I infiltrated them," I say proudly. "I'm your inside man, well, girl."

"No, no, no." She shakes her head, sending her ponytail whipping through the air. "When they call you, say you'll meet them at Kira Cornish's residence. Then my men and I will move in while you stay safe and sound in your hotel."

I roll my eyes. "David will never fall for that. He'll cancel the heist. I'll fly back to Phoenix. You won't be able to connect with him." Plus, I'm so not leaving the mystery in the hands of Detective Garcia and the Beverly Hills PD.

She folds her arms. A variety of expressions cross her face as she realizes she's totally backed into a corner. Finally, she puffs out a breath of air. "As soon as you hear from them, call me. I'll give you my cell number. No delays. A police car will follow you to the scene."

"I can even call you again with details once we're set up at Kira Cornish's," I say. "I'm the lookout girl. I'll be disguised as a dog walker. So I'll contact you from the street."

"Where's your dad?" the detective asks, her arms still crossed. "He needs to be in on this operation."

"I'm out if he's in." I cross my arms too.

The two of us face off, like we're in an old Western movie.

Finally, the detective's arms drop to her sides. I'm a teen; I have staying power in face-offs against adults.

"Look," I say. "Nothing can go wrong. I'll call you before I leave the hotel with Lorraine, Stef and the others. You follow behind in an unmarked car. I'll call you again from outside Kira Cornish's house when I'm walking a dog on the street. I'll relay any additional info about the heist that I picked up during the van ride."

"I don't like this," the detective says. "You're thirteen."

I wave a hand in the air, dismissing her worries. "But I'm mature for my age." I think back briefly to other mysteries I've been involved in. This is the safest I've ever felt. I even have police backup. "I've never been so well covered. Nothing can go wrong."

Detective Garcia crosses her arms again. "Sherry, when you've been on the force as long as I have, you know there's still plenty that can go wrong."

chapter
thirty-one

Back at the hotel, Junie's waiting for me in the lobby. So is Leah. "How'd it go with Detective Garcia?" they both ask, which is really weird given that Junie can't even hear Leah.

I give them the scoop. "Junie, I'm texting you Detective Garcia's cell number in case I have to call or text you to get in touch with her while I'm out in the field."

"Take me with you to Kira Cornish's," Leah says. "You don't have to deal with the bad guys all by yourself."

"Thanks, Leah. I know you're worried about me," I say. "But I have to be totally alone. I can't have a ghost by my side. Please understand."

Leah sighs. "I understand. Your mom gave me some

tips for trying to cross thresholds. I'm going to go practice." The smell of root beer disappears as she flies away.

I tell Junie what Leah's up to.

Junie finishes assigning a speed-dial number to Detective Garcia. "Want to check out the Marilyn Monroe stuff? Here and in the Blossom Ballroom?"

The hotel has begun decorating for the Marilyn Monroe look-alike contest that's happening tomorrow. In the lobby, there are huge Marilyn Monroe movie posters on easels. A banner with details of the evening dangles over the check-in counter. In the ballroom, every corner has a white screen for presenting various Marilyn Monroe movies throughout the evening. The walls are covered with photos of her. There are still some gaps for more photos.

But the real place of interest is in the middle of the room. There are no chairs. There's no table. It's just a space. An empty space.

"The mirror must be going right here." I tap my foot on the tile floor.

Junie stands in the space. "Weird to think that tomorrow night Marilyn Monroe might actually show up in a mirror. On this very spot."

"I hope it works out for my mother and she learns something about Marilyn's death."

We wander back to the lobby to look at the movie posters.

We're in front of the poster for *Gentlemen Prefer Blondes,* reading the caption: *Two showgirls, Lorelei Lee (Marilyn Monroe) and Dorothy Shaw (Jane Russell), travel to Paris in search of true love and marriage, 1953.*

"I should write an article on Marilyn Monroe. I could write about tomorrow evening, about the ghost mirror, her mysterious death, her movies." Junie's jotting down ideas in her notebook.

"I'll ask my mom for info for you too. She could write an entire book about Marilyn Monroe."

"Sounds exactly like my mom," says a voice next to me.

I turn. Standing by my elbow, reading the movie facts, is Mark.

I introduce him to Junie.

"Do you think Marilyn Monroe will show up tomorrow night?" he asks.

"Hopefully." Junie sticks her notebook in her backpack. "Look at all the trouble the hotel's going to for her."

"Do you believe in ghosts?" I ask him.

He doesn't respond right away, like he's really considering my question. "I don't know," he answers finally. "I don't personally have any experience with a ghost, but I don't want to say a definite no." He flashes a grin. "Will you accept that the jury's out?"

"Sure," I say.

Junie's phone pings. She totally focuses in on the message. It must be from Nick. She starts thumb-tapping a response, then stops and glances at me and Mark. "This is going to last a while. I'm grabbing a seat over there." She gestures toward the indoor fountain.

For once, I don't mind that Nick is texting her. I'm cool with a little conversation time with Mark Peña and my pitter-pattering heart. A bubble—like in a comic strip—blinks in my brain. Inside the bubble is one word: "Josh." I shake my head and the bubble pops. If Josh can hold hands with a high-school girl at the mall, I'm good with chatting with a cute guy.

"Where are you from?" Mark asks.

I tell him. "And you?"

"Flagstaff."

We high-five. "Arizona rules!" I say.

"You wanna get a soda in 25 Degrees?" Mark asks.

My heart has gone from pitter-patter to actually skipping around like a rubber ball on an elementary school playground. "Yeah, just let me tell Junie."

I want to race over to where she's flaked out on a leather chair, but force myself to walk at a reasonable speed. "Mark and I are grabbing a soda at 25 Degrees."

"I'll stay here. Text me if he turns out to be boring or whatever and you need me to save you." Junie smiles. "But he seems really nice."

Mark and I slide into a booth, order and start talking. And talking. And talking. We have literally tons in common. Video games. Funny movies. Stepparent. Pesky younger brother. We both didn't like Taco Magnifico.

Mark checks the screen of his phone. "Oh, wow, we've been talking for a couple of hours. I better get going." He punches a few buttons. "You wanna exchange numbers? Maybe hit Ripley's Believe It or Not together? Or that Mexican restaurant you mentioned?"

I've just entered him on my contact list when my phone rings.

"You're the One," by the Boyfriends, blasts from my palm. The ringtone that pumps up my heart like I'm jogging the mile in PE class.

Josh is calling!

chapter
thirty-two

Mark heads to the elevator. I dash into the lobby to find Junie, who's scribbling in her notebook.

"Junie! Junie!" I wave my phone. "Josh called."

She closes her notebook and slides it into her backpack. "And?"

"I couldn't answer. I was with Mark."

"You gonna call him back now?"

The lobby is noisy with guests chatting and hotel workers moving Marilyn Monroe paraphernalia. "No."

She stands and takes my arm. "Let's go up to our room."

A breeze swirls around me. "Sherry!" my mom

says. "Sherry! Finally, I got a tip on how to lure Marilyn here!"

"What?" I say. I turn to Junie. "My mom knows how to get Marilyn to show up."

"Artichokes!" my mother says.

"Artichokes?" I say.

"In 1947, Marilyn Monroe was crowned the very first Miss California Artichoke Queen in Castroville, California," my mom says. "And since then, she's felt a connection to the thistle."

I repeat the odd trivia to Junie, who immediately pulls out her notebook and writes down the info. "So, do you need us to find a grocery store and buy an artichoke by tomorrow evening?" I ask my mom.

"No, Mrs. Howard's taking care of it."

"Mrs. Howard?" I gulp. "She's coming back out here?"

"Turns out she's a huge Marilyn Monroe fan," my mother says. "You're doing fine, right? I checked the World Wide Web for the Dead, and there's not anything recent about you."

"Absolutely everything's übercopa with me. No problems. Not anticipating any." My arms are outstretched with my palms facing up, like my life's an open book.

"Mrs. Howard arrives tomorrow afternoon. She wants me to introduce her to some of the L.A. ghosts I've met," Mom says. "So let's rendezvous in the lobby at nine."

"Tomorrow evening, nine o'clock work for you, Junie?" I ask.

"Sure," she says. "I'm excited."

Fingers crossed tomorrow evening isn't heist time.

"Thanks for keeping your behavior squeaky clean," Mom says. "I know Mrs. Howard can be tough. I'm just looking forward to you and me teaming up again." The scent of coffee weakens as my mother floats away. "See you tomorrow night."

Even ghost mothers can dole out the guilt.

Junie and I are the only passengers in the elevator. I check my phone. "Josh didn't leave a message."

"You want me to wait in the hall while you call him?" Junie asks.

"No, I need your moral support. I don't know what to say to him." I chew on my bottom lip. "I mean, he was at the mall, holding hands with another girl."

"Maybe he's ready to get back together?" Junie says. "Maybe a couple of hours with whoever she was convinced him that you're irreplaceable."

Definitely a possibility. This could be the make-up call that will patch the holes in my heart. Then again, maybe he left a video game at my house and wants it back.

Walking down the hall, Junie shakes her head slowly, her red hair swaying. "Poor Josh. I bet he misses you so badly." Her eyes are misty.

How very unexpected that Junie and I have

switched places. She's more romantic than me. Nick is turning her 4.0 brain to mush. She should've entered an essay on true love in *Hollywood Girl*'s competition. What's next in my life? A fancy scientific calculator?

I flop down on the bed, my phone next to me. Despite all the scratches, its silver case gleams.

I stare at it. I want to call. But I don't want to call. My hands are sweaty.

Junie hands me a 7Up from the mini fridge. "If anyone can pull off this phone call, it's you, Sherry." She fluffs up the pillows behind me. "You wrote a winning essay on love. You know all the advice Dear Elle's given for the past couple of years. You're über-prepared."

Then why is my heart throwing itself against my rib cage? I press the cold soda can against my forehead and close my eyes. I think about all the Dear Elle columns I've read. I think about my essay where I said sweaty hands and a pounding heart are signs of true love and shouldn't be ignored. Is it even true? I suck in a deep calming breath.

I speed-dial Josh.

He picks up fast. "Hi, Sherry!"

"Hey, Josh." I get the words out between heartbeats. "You called?"

"Yeah, uh. So, how's the trip?"

"Good." With each sentence, I'm less nervous.

"Nick told me you found a mystery. Is it working out okay?"

"Yeah, sure." And now that I'm not so nervous, something really weird is going on. I'm getting mad.

"I've been playing lots of water polo. With extra-tough practices. Like eggbeater while holding up a five-gallon jug filled with water."

Eggbeater? Oh yeah, some sort of strenuous leg-kicking move. "Sounds tiring." Of course, solving a mystery and keeping it secret from your ghost mom and juggling your corny dad and making sure your best friend and your new ghost friend get along? That's no walk in the park.

"Coach is working us hard, trying to train us so we'll make it all the way to league championships."

"So, Brianna saw you at the mall." The words just pop out. Unplanned. But, now that I've said them, it seems right. I mean, pretending it didn't happen is mean to me and to the other girl.

Junie slaps a hand over her mouth.

"I know," Josh says. "I'm sorry."

I wait to see what else he'll say.

Junie's leaning toward me, anxious.

"Listen." Josh clears his throat. "It was nothing. Really. I barely know Olivia."

Olivia? So the high school girl in the expensive denim skirt has a name. "You were holding hands," I say flatly. "And swinging your arms."

Junie's head drops to her chest.

"I gotta go," I say. "Junie's waiting for me. And you know how impatient she can get."

"Hey," Junie says.

Josh and I say quick goodbyes and click off.

Her head tilted to one side, Junie stares at me. "Somehow I don't think that's how Dear Elle would've handled the phone call."

"Here's the deal, Junie," I say. "I don't think Dear Elle is such an outstanding love expert."

Junie watches me carefully.

"I could've gotten better advice from my grandpa. He's been with my grandma forever. He obviously knows something."

Junie's still watching me.

"Anyway, I have a ton on my plate right now." I pop open the soda and sip. "Like what am I supposed to do if Stef texts me for the heist right when I'm sightseeing with my dad? I can't just say, 'Excuse me, Dad. Please drive me back to the hotel, where I'll catch a ride with a teen burglary ring. I'm part of the sting operation to take them down.' And what if the heist happens tomorrow evening during the Marilyn Monroe event?"

Junie's tongue pokes out between her lips. After a few minutes of intense concentration, she says, "There's no point worrying whether the heist is planned for tomorrow evening. If it is, it is. And we'll figure out at that time how you can sneak away from Mrs. Howard and your mom." Junie sits next to me on the bed and we lean against each other, shoulder to shoulder.

"But handling your dad?" She snaps her fingers. "Leave it to me."

thirty-three

The next morning my dad is up bright and early like a bird. He knocks on the adjoining door.

Junie cracks the door. "Shhh. Sherry's feeling under the weather."

"What? Sherry's sick?" My dad peers in. "Is she still in bed?"

We purposely left the lights off, and our room is dim.

"She's on the couch," Junie says in a low voice. "For the day."

"For the day?" My dad shoulders open the door. "We'll call Paula. She'll know exactly what to do." He fumbles in his pocket for his phone. "She's amazing that way. Even long-distance."

"Paula can't fix this," Junie says. "Sherry talked to Josh last night. They're, well, not getting along."

"Of course they're not getting along. They've broken up." He rubs his forehead. "Isn't that the definition of 'broken up'? Not getting along?"

"She needs a day to own the heartache and process it."

"A whole day?" Dad's so out of his league. "I want to take you girls shopping on Rodeo Drive."

I groan. I'm giving up shopping on Rodeo Drive!

Dad comes over. "Are you okay, pumpkin?"

"I'll be fine," I say hoarsely.

"Would food help?" he asks. "A breakfast burrito from across the street?"

"Definitely." I sit straight up.

"Sherry?" Junie rubs my back. Her eyes are wide, sending me a settle-down-be-less-enthusiastic message. "Maybe some food in an hour or so?"

"Tell me what to do," Dad says. "I can't leave you in here for hours. Ginger ale? A thermometer? Read out loud to you?"

"No, no, Dad. Don't give up touristy fun in Southern California. Just because I need a day of depression." I wipe under my eyes where tears would pool, if there were tears. "I'll only feel worse if I rob you of a day too."

"Seriously, Mr. Baldwin, go do something cool.

Otherwise, Sherry'll end up taking two days of depression," Junie says. "I'll stay with her and catch up on my writing for the school paper."

"Really?" My poor dad looks completely confused, like he's a gerbil trapped in a maze.

Junie opens the adjoining door. "Did you know the Comedy Store is offering stand-up classes? Sherry would feel better if you did something like that."

"I would," I say.

"Really?" He shuffles through to his room. "I'll leave my cell on loud. And I'll call you every few hours."

"Bye, Dad. Love you." I raise a hand and wave weakly. "Thanks for understanding about this day of depression."

I loll around for about an hour while Junie's hunched over her keyboard.

"Junie, I'm bored out of my mind," I say. "Let's go hang out at the pool and get something to eat."

"Sure. If you're over your depression." She giggles.

We change into our bikinis. I grab the nail polish supplies. We manage to snag chaise longues again. We relax in the sun and do each other's nails.

My mom breezes in. "Where's your dad?"

"Taking stand-up comedy classes." I roll over on my back.

"Excellent!" my mom says. "He has such a great sense of humor."

"Uh, Mom"—I frown—"have you forgotten all his lame jokes?"

She sighs. "No, Sherry, your dad's humor is something I always appreciated about him."

Parents!

After my mom takes off, Junie and I trek across the street to the Mexican place. I branch out and order a California burrito. It's überdelicious with carne asada, cheese and fries.

After lunch, Leah joins us. We order a comedy movie to the room, which she watches and actually laughs at. After she leaves, Junie and I nap and text back and forth with Brianna. All in all, it's a mucho enjoyable day.

Finally, I'm dozing off for a second nap around three o'clock, when my phone pings with a text from Stef.

```
<b in pkg lot in 15>
```

It's on.

chapter
thirty-four

I call Detective Garcia. "They want me in the parking lot in fifteen minutes."

"Be careful," she says tersely.

I change into a cute dog-walking outfit: denim shorts, patterned red-and-blue T-shirt with scoop neck, sandals.

I toss my phone back in my purse, redo my mascara, then open the hotel room door. I stick my nose out into the hall, sniffing like an anteater. No root beer gloss.

Junie and I stride to the elevator. Everything about me is alert. I'm like an appliance, plugged in, always on, with a low buzz.

Downstairs, we separate. Junie goes to the sitting

area in the lobby. I push open the glass doors to the parking lot and step into the hot sun and an undercover sting.

A shiny gray van pulls up. A magnet sign on the passenger door reads BEVERLY HILLS POOL SERVICE. The side door slides open. I enter.

I briefly think about how my dad would kill me if he knew I was getting into this van. But at least Detective Garcia has my back.

Alone at the front, David's got the wheel. "Grab a seat and buckle up."

Lorraine and Stef sit on the middle bench. A small black poodle lies at their feet.

I plunk down in the back, next to Taylor. She hooks a strand of purple hair behind her ear, gives me the briefest of nods and stares out the window.

"Hi, Sherry," Lorraine says. "Adorable shirt."

"Thanks." She and Stef are in jeans, two layers of tank tops, and sneakers. They must coordinate their outfits every day. Taylor is also wearing jeans, but with a solid black crew-neck T-shirt.

We take off from the parking lot at a normal speed. Everything about this operation is normal. It's all about not sticking out and calling attention to ourselves: a clean pool-company van keeping to the speed limit with non-scruffy passengers seat-belted in. These guys are pros.

The poodle rubs against my legs. "What's your name?" I lean over and scratch her neck.

"Dorothy," Taylor answers in a monotone, still gazing out the window.

Dorothy jumps up beside me and lies down. Obviously, she's attracted to noncriminals.

In Beverly Hills, I recognize a few of the streets and houses from the tour. We approach the hill leading up to Kira Cornish's house. My hand grips the edge of the seat. This is it.

David clicks on his signal. And turns in the opposite direction!

"Excuse me," I call out. "You just missed the turn to Kira Cornish's."

"Kira's at home," Lorraine says. "Word is she's got the stomach flu."

"More like cosmetic surgery," Taylor mutters.

"We're hitting Sarah Sutherland's instead," Stef says.

Ack! Eek! Ike! I'm trapped in a van with David and his teen thieves! And Detective Garcia is headed to the wrong location!

I take a deep breath. I'll call the detective when I'm walking Dorothy. Everything will be fine. Everything is still on track. So why is my heart pounding?

David cuts the engine by the curb of a large two-story white stucco house. It has fat round columns and a couple of armless statues in front.

He turns around. "Pass me your cells, girls."

Lorraine, Stef and Taylor act like this is no big deal, just your run-of-the-mill procedure for heist day.

"Sherry, your cell." David holds out his hand.

"But I need mine," I say, trying not to look as nervous as I feel. "Remember? I'm the dog walker. I have to call you if I see something suspicious."

David unzips his backpack, tosses in the girls' phones and pulls out three walkie-talkies.

"Give me your phone, Sherry," he says in a no-nonsense voice. Negotiations are obviously not his strong suit.

I have zero choice. I pass the phone to Stef, who passes it to David. My phone, which has Detective Garcia's name and number in it. Plus, she was my last call.

"No cells because I don't want anyone taking photos in the house. Next thing I know, they'll be plastered all over the Internet," David says. "Here's a walkie-talkie for inside the house." He tosses one to Stef. "A walkie-talkie for the van." He places one on the dash. "And a walkie-talkie for the dog walker." He tosses the last one to Taylor.

Ack! Eek! Ike! "But *I'm* the dog walker," I say.

David gestures with his shoulder to Stef. "Tell her to shut up."

"Taylor convinced David it's her turn to walk the

dog." Stef's large round eyes tell me to quit making comments.

A little smile sneaks onto Taylor's face.

I have no cell. The heist is at a different location. I'm off dog-walking duty. I don't even know exactly what I *am* doing now. Other than breaking into a house and robbing it. I'll be back in the limelight on the World Wide Web for the Dead. The Academy will hate me forever and never let me work with my mom again. I literally feel all the blood drain from my face. What else can go wrong?

My cell phone rings.

David throws me my cell. "Answer it on speaker-phone."

I'm shaking.

"Hi, Sherry. It's Sam."

My little brother, who rarely calls me, couldn't have picked a worse time.

"Hey, Sam," I say. "Can I call you back later?"

"Act normal," David whispers. "Talk for a minute."

"Sherry, I'm really sorry. But I don't know what to do about your fish. They're acting crazy. I swear I didn't overfeed them." Sam's talking fast and nervous.

"What're they doing?"

"I think they're gonna kill each other." Sam's voice chokes.

"What're they doing?" I repeat.

"They're going after each other," Sam says. "Paula called the pet store, but they didn't have any advice for us."

David makes a cutting sign across his throat. "Enough," he whispers. "Tell him they're just fish and end the conversation."

"They're just fish, Sam. I'll call back."

There's stunned silence from Sam. "They're just fish?"

"They're just fish. Bye." Freaking out, freaking out, freaking out.

David snaps my phone shut. He throws a leash to Taylor. "Do your thing."

She clips the walkie-talkie to her waistband, then hooks the leash around Dorothy's collar and squeezes by me. Through the van's windshield, we watch her sashaying down the street, letting Dorothy sniff here and there.

An older woman with silver hair and a cane hobbles toward her. They chat. Taylor points to Sarah Sutherland's house and to the van, then holds Dorothy for the woman to pat. I've never seen Taylor so animated. Completely different from how she was at the library and in the van. She's a good actor.

After the woman limps off, Taylor's voice crackles in on the walkie-talkie. "The coast is clear."

"Stef and Lorraine, I want you to find a painting of a silver mine. Should be a decent size. It's worth a mint," David says. Then he reels off two other artists' names that are meaningless to me. "Those paintings are worth something too. Although the silver mine painting?" He gives a low whistle.

"Sherry, you locate a key, then pick up electronics like laptops and iPads." David hands us all disposable gloves, which we pull on immediately. "There's no security system," he says. "When Taylor scoped out the place this morning, the side door was unlocked. Try that first. If it's locked, go through a back window." He points. "Pile the stuff outside the side door. I'll pull into the driveway for fast loading."

He looks at me. "If I give a signal on the walkie-talkie that you gotta get out, you obey. Pronto. You get caught in Sarah Sutherland's house? Well, just think of how famous you'll be back in Phoenix."

"But I so don't do famous," I wail.

David frowns, then jerks his head at me, Lorraine and Stef. "Go!"

I plod up the drive, several steps behind Lorraine and Stef. The side door is open and we scoot in.

The ground floor is a huge living room, a huge dining room, a huge kitchen and a huge bathroom. I stand in the living room, in the middle of rich.

Lorraine pockets a small wooden elephant from the metal and glass coffee table. "Love this."

"Let's start on the top floor," Stef says to her.

"Look around on this level for a key," Lorraine says to me. "Maybe in the kitchen."

They skip up the stairs, chattering like they're at the mall on a shopping trip.

"Sarah's most recent movie was *Baltimore Blues,* right?" Stef says.

"Yeah," Lorraine says.

"'Cause she looked like about our size in that flick," Stef says. "I could use some new jeans."

My hands shoved deep in my pockets, I walk from the living room to the dining room to the kitchen to the bathroom and back to the living room. I can't bring myself to touch a thing. It's so weird to be in a movie star's house. On the end table by the couch is a copy of Dear Elle's book. In the kitchen, there's the same kind of light green juice glass that we have at home. Maybe celebrities are just like ordinary people.

The more I wander around, the more nauseated I feel. This really sucks. A burglary is going down. And I'm in the middle of it. Without my cell, I can't contact Detective Garcia or Junie or my dad for help. And I promised Mrs. Howard and my mother that I wouldn't get involved with this case. I'll be dead meat with the Academy.

"Did you find a key yet, Sherry?" Stef calls from the landing at the top of the stairs.

I look up. "No."

"Get on it!" Stef says. "We need you. A couple of these paintings are too heavy for just Lorraine and me."

She's holding the edge of a picture frame. Two stairs below her, Lorraine's hanging on to the bottom half of the painting. "Come on, Lorraine. You know how impatient David gets," Stef says.

Lorraine's walking backward. "This isn't easy, Stef. The floor's slippery."

"Sherry, get up here and help," Stef orders.

I brush my gloved hands against my shorts, take a deep breath and start climbing.

Lorraine's left foot dangles in the air, between stairs. Her toe draws circles, trying to find solid ground. She teeters, listing.

"Sherry!" Stef yells.

I bound up, two steps at a time.

At the last second, Lorraine catches her balance. But she pulls hard on the frame, yanking the picture from Stef's grip.

The painting spins from Lorraine's fingertips.

Toward me.

I reach out my arms. The painting lurches at me. My left hand makes contact with the frame. My fingers curl and hang on tight. My right hand misses the edge and hits the canvas.

Rip!

My hand goes through.

Lorraine and Stef arrive on the stair above me. They pull the picture off my arm.

They stare at the ruined painting, their mouths open and their skin greenish.

"David's going to go ballistic," Lorraine whispers.

"Idiot!" Stef says. "You tore through the middle of the mine shaft. You destroyed a *priceless* painting."

"We can't give it to him in this condition," Lorraine says. "Let's put it back in the room where we found it and tell him it just wasn't here."

Stef frowns. "He'll hear about it on the news or something. Our best bet is to tell him the truth. Sherry wrecked the painting."

A shiver snakes through me, like someone injected ice water in my veins. "It wasn't really my fault."

"It was an accident, Stef." A thin blue vein beats against Lorraine's pale neck. "You know what David'll do."

"My point exactly." Stef's lips are a grim line. "That's why we're throwing her to the dogs."

"Sorry, Sherry," Lorraine whispers. She really does look sorry.

Stef and Lorraine cart the picture downstairs and out through the side door.

"What are we supposed to do now?" Lorraine says, reentering the house. "No way we can carry those last two paintings down by ourselves."

"She *has* to help," Stef says. "Sherry, if we get the paintings down the stairs without messing up, we'll ask David to go easy on you."

"Like I have any choice," I mutter.

"That's true." Stef starts up the stairs. "You don't."

Stef and I follow. At the top, we hang a right and head down a long hall to an almost empty office. There's a desk and a chair and a couple of paintings leaning against the wall, waiting to be hung.

Taking baby steps, the three of us maneuver the largest painting all the way down the stairs without mishap. We prop it outside, by the door, and trudge back inside for the last painting. I think we're all sweating.

Cackle. Cackle.

David's voice blasts over the walkie-talkie. "What happened to this painting?"

"Sherry," Stef responds.

"Sherry!" David yells through the walkie-talkie. "Where's Sherry? Get me Sherry! I'm coming in!"

"He's coming in?" Lorraine grabs Stef's hand. They back away from the door.

"He never risks coming in a house," Stef says. "Too serious for him if he gets caught. He's an adult."

"I told you he'd go ballistic," Lorraine says, swallowing.

They keep backing up. All the way to the top of the

stairs, where they sit. "You're on your own for this one, Sherry," Stef says.

The walkie-talkie cackling is loud now, just on the other side of the door.

I'm shaking like I've got a huge fever.

The doorknob turns.

The door cracks open.

chapter
thirty-five

Suddenly, a strong smell of coffee, burnt sugar and root beer storms by me. Mom! Mrs. Howard! Leah!

The door slams shut.

"Sherry!" David rattles the doorknob. "Open up!"

"He'll never get past us," Mom says.

Lorraine gasps. "It's almost like a force field won't let him in."

"You watch too much TV," Stef says. "We probably locked it by mistake."

I smile to myself. It's a force field of three ghosts.

A siren wails. Louder and louder. Then stops.

Outside the door, I hear Detective Garcia. She reads David his rights. "Cuff him and take him to the car, Detective Bowen," she says.

Detective Garcia steps into the house. Her hair is pulled tightly back in a ponytail. No wispy, flyaway hairs today. With steely eyes, she stares at each of us.

"The detective's treating you like one of the gang to protect you," Mom says. "She doesn't want the others to know you're the mole."

"Just play along, Sherry," Mrs. Howard says.

Officer Mullins enters. Not even the slightest recognition crosses his face when he glances at me. Everyone in L.A.'s an actor.

Detective Garcia unlocks handcuffs from her belt. "How old are you girls?"

"Just fifteen." Lorraine's eyes are on the cuffs, and her lower lip quivers.

The detective glares at Stef.

"I'm fifteen too," she says in a small voice. "What's going to happen to us?"

The detective ignores her and snaps cuffs on Lorraine. Officer Mullins cuffs Stef.

"Because they're minors, we have to transport them back to the station in a separate vehicle from the male suspect, right?" Officer Mullins says.

"Correct," Detective Garcia says.

Tears spill from Lorraine's and Stef's eyes. "My dad's going to kill me," Lorraine says in a strangled voice.

Detective Garcia turns to me. "You look familiar. Have I apprehended you before?"

"Uh, no." I gulp.

"Good job staying in character," Leah says.

"What's your name?" she barks.

"Sherry Baldwin." I stare at the floor.

"As in 'Sherlock Baldwin'?" The detective steps toward me. "Aka Sticky Fingers Baldwin, Arizona's infamous tween thief?"

I nod, weakly.

"Sherry, you are so a natural actress," Leah says.

"She is good," Mom says proudly.

"This better get the proper spin on the World Wide Web for the Dead," Mrs. Howard says.

Mullins wrenches my arms behind my back and cuffs me.

Detective Garcia pulls her cell off her thick black belt. "I'm telling Bowen to take the male suspect to the station. He can use one of the squad cars we brought here, get the paperwork done, then transport the suspect to jail." She starts punching numbers into her phone. "You take Sticky Fingers to the station in the remaining squad car. Run her through the computer and find out what she's wanted for in Arizona." The detective stops stabbing the number pad. "And, Mullins, Sticky Fingers may look young and naïve, but she's dirty. She's really bad news."

"What're you gonna do, Detective?" Officer Mullins asks.

"I'll call for another unit. Then I'll transport these

two"—the detective jerks her head at Stef and Lorraine—"to the station, write up my report and escort them over to juvenile hall."

Lorraine and Stef start crying.

"Plus, I want the van impounded." Garcia ignores the girls and presses the cell to her ear, waiting for Bowen to pick up.

"Come with me," Mullins says roughly, yanking my arm. He leads me to a police car parked out of view. I can smell the ghosts trailing along with us.

"I'm so proud of you, Sherry," Mom says. "Although we need to talk about the danger you put yourself in."

"Meeting poolside back at the hotel," Mrs. Howard says.

"Including me?" Leah asks.

"Of course," Mrs. Howard answers. "Sherry, we'll see you at the hotel." The aromas of coffee, cinnamon buns and root beer gloss waft away.

Officer Mullins and I reach the car. Dad's sitting in the front. Junie's in the back. The officer unlocks my cuffs and hands me my cell phone. He shakes my hand. "Great job, Sherry. It's an honor working with you. Detective Garcia wanted to pass along that you have a bright future in law enforcement ahead of you."

"Thanks."

"And, Sherry," he adds, "we've already been in

touch with Sarah Sutherland. The paintings were heavily insured."

"Yay!" I say.

My dad steps out of the car and sweeps me up in a tight hug. "Sherry, I'm relieved you're okay. But you took an incredible risk getting involved in all this. I can't believe you got in that van."

"I know. I'm sorry." He releases me, and I slide in next to Junie. We high-five.

While we're riding back to the hotel, I get some of the gaps filled in.

"Okay," I say. "I have a million questions. For starters, how'd you figure out where the heist was?"

"Well, when you never called or showed at Kira Cornish's, Detective Garcia knew something was wrong," Junie says. "She contacted me, but I couldn't tell her anything because I hadn't heard from you."

"David took my cell," I say.

"Sam phoned me after talking to you," Dad says. "He was worried because you were so callous about your fish. At first, I thought maybe it was all tied in with your day of depression, but then Junie spilled the beans about the investigation."

"Sorry, Dad," I say. "I figured you wouldn't let me go undercover."

He nods, but I can tell he's still not thrilled about that part.

"Detective Garcia wanted to let you in on the sting, but I wouldn't let her," I say.

"We'll talk about this later." Dad's expression is solemn.

"How did Detective Garcia figure out we were robbing Sarah Sutherland's?" I ask.

"After your last visit to her office, the detective compiled a list of all the Raccoonites, with a subset of those who are Hollywood success stories," Junie explains. "Then it was a question of checking out the few on her list who hadn't been burglarized yet."

"Smart," I say.

Back at the hotel, Officer Mullins pumps my hand again.

"I think room service is in order," Dad says. "After a day like today."

"Sounds great. I'll meet you guys upstairs. I need a little time to myself," I say. "I have a meeting by the pool with Mrs. Howard, Mom and Leah," I whisper to Junie.

The lobby is already filling with people for tonight's Marilyn Monroe look-alike contest. Many are in costume. I pick my way through the people, then take the outside walkway to the pool area. A nervous feeling gnaws at my stomach. It comes from crossing Mrs. Howard.

From the smell of it, the three ghosts are already at

a back corner table when I arrive. Mrs. Howard is a big blurry ball by the open umbrella. I pull out a chair.

"Way to save the day," Mom whispers in my ear.

I nod.

The pool area isn't crowded, but it isn't empty either. I hold my cell to my ear, pretending I'm engaged in conversation with a live person.

"Sherry, you've done it again," Mrs. Howard says.

I nod, not exactly sure if this is good or bad.

"You're already making headlines on the World Wide Web for the Dead," she says.

"Oh yeah," I say, still noncommittal. Is she mad? Proud? She's the moodiest, most impossible-to-read ghost around.

"Leah's mentioned too," Mrs. Howard says.

"Really? I am?" Leah squeals. "Does it say anything about how great a help I was on the case? Does it talk about the movie I was in before I died? Am I getting famous?"

"There's nothing but good about you, Leah." Mrs. Howard oozes cinnamon and sugar.

"How did you know I was at Sarah Sutherland's?" I ask. "And that I needed help?"

"That would be me." No doubt Leah is raising a hand. The scent of root beer strengthens as she settles near me. "When I saw Junie all alone in the lobby, I guessed something was wrong."

"So you hung around Junie and eavesdropped on her phone calls with Detective Garcia?" I say.

"Basically," Leah says. "Like a stakeout in the lobby."

"Good thinking, Leah," I say.

"Leah hunted me down when she realized you were in trouble," Mom says.

"Sherry, honey," Mrs. Howard drawls, "everyone at the Academy is very proud of you."

Phew.

"Can I tell her, Mrs. Howard? Can I tell her?" I bet Leah's bouncing up and down like a kid at a birthday party.

"Certainly, dear," Mrs. Howard says.

"I applied for a position with the Academy of Spirits," Leah says proudly. "As your partner."

"Very cool," I say. And I mean it.

"Leah's coming back to Phoenix with us," Mrs. Howard says. "But I'm taking her over to see her family first."

"Could I have a word with you, Mrs. Howard?" I ask.

chapter
thirty-six

I t's nine o'clock and time for the Marilyn Monroe look-alike contest.

Dad, Junie and I head downstairs. Junie and I are wearing Marilyn Monroe T-shirts that we bought across the street at a souvenir store.

The elevator doors open to the sound of Marilyn Monroe belting out "Diamonds Are a Girl's Best Friend." The Blossom Ballroom is filled with Marilyn look-alikes. There's a sea of blond wigs. The most popular outfits copy the short white halter dress from *The Seven Year Itch* movie and the long rhinestone-covered evening gown Marilyn wore when she sang "Happy Birthday" to President Kennedy.

Dad wanders around the periphery of the room, texting photos back to The Ruler.

"Isn't this amazing?" Mom swoops in beside me.

"Totally," I say. "Where are Mrs. Howard and Leah?"

"Somewhere around here, working on crossing thresholds," Mom says.

"What's the deal with them?" I ask. "Why is Mrs. Howard so crazy about her?"

"I'm not sure, but Mrs. Howard has a very long and complicated past," Mom says. "I think Leah reminds her a little of herself at a certain age."

"Well, while I think Leah will be fun to work with, you'll always be my first choice."

"Sherry, you are so sweet." She touches my cheek. "It'll all pan out. And, at this point, I'm still on loan to the foreign Academy."

"Sherry!" Dad's waving his phone at me. "Phone call!" He starts wending his way through a pack of Marilyn Monroes.

"And thank you for setting up Real Time through Mrs. Howard for your father and me," Mom says.

"When are you going to do it?" I ask, all excited.

"Now," Mom says.

"Really?" I suck in a breath.

Dad presses his phone into my palm. "Paula has amazing news."

"Hello, Paula," I say.

"Here's Sam," she says. "He wanted to be the one to tell you."

I follow my dad, who goes into 25 Degrees and sits in a booth, his face to me. I stand at the door, watching.

"Sherry?" Sam says.

"Just a sec, Sam," I say.

The waiter brings Dad water. He points to something on the menu, and the waiter leaves. Dad raises the glass to his lips, then sets it down, smiling across the table, like he sees someone there. His clasped hands, relaxed shoulders and lips turned up in a content grin all tell me Real Time has begun. Dad won't remember it, but he'll carry the good feelings from it forever.

I turn away. It's private. "What's going on, Sam?"

"I didn't hurt your fish. I didn't do anything to your fish." His voice squeaks with excitement. "No one did."

"Are they acting normal today?" I ask.

"Nope," Sam says. "Not at all."

"What are you talking about?"

"Cindy laid eggs!" Sam shouts. "All over the bottom of the aquarium."

A proud parental feeling flows through me. Cindy laid eggs. We have a fry. Bala sharks almost never, ever lay eggs in captivity. But my fish are so happy and healthy and in love. They just couldn't help themselves. It all goes back to my essay. When you're in love, everything in your life falls into line. Pimples clear up. Math homework makes sense. Your room stays clean.

Junie and I mill around. At ten o'clock, the hotel staff wheel a dolly into the middle of the Blossom Ballroom. On the dolly sits a squat mirror, the kind you find on a bathroom counter. The mirror is framed by ornate silver curlicues.

The smell of coffee breezes around me. "Sherry," my mother says, "Mrs. Howard left an artichoke under the table with the guest book. I don't want to carry it because it'll look like it's floating through the air."

I tell Junie, and we skip over to get it.

We crowd around the mirror, along with many Marilyn Monroes and my dad. I balance the artichoke so that it's leaning on the frame.

I sniff. "No Mrs. Howard or Leah."

"I don't know where they are," my mother says. "I'm worried they'll miss Marilyn's appearance."

"Hi, Sherry," says a voice at my shoulder. "I thought I might find you here."

"Hi, Mark!"

"Any sign of her yet?" he asks.

I shake my head, staring intently at the mirror, willing Marilyn's ghost to appear.

"Want to hang out tomorrow?" he asks. "It's my last day."

"Definitely. I just have to check with my dad."

"And your mother," my mom says in my ear.

"Sure thing," I say under my breath.

"Hi, Mark," Junie says.

The hotel dims the lights until the entire focus of the room is on the little mirror. All goes silent.

The smell of cinnamon rolls hovers above me. Mrs. Howard has arrived.

I sniff. The room is filled with a lot of different smells. French fries, lavender, flowers. A host of ghosts have arrived to greet Marilyn.

The scent of root beer rolls in next to me. "That's not the mirror I saw her in," Leah says. "The right one must still be in the basement."

"Downstairs, ghosts," Mrs. Howard commands.

"Did you hear that, Sherry?" my mom whispers.

"Got it," I say quickly. I scoop up the artichoke.

"Junie"—I tug on her elbow—"can I talk with you?" She nods.

"Later, gator," I say to Mark.

He smiles.

When we reach the outskirts of the crowd, I say, "Junie, they brought up the wrong mirror. The right one's still in the basement."

We barrel down. A dusty cloth is lifted from a plain full-length mirror. I place the artichoke next to it.

The mirror goes dark and cloudy, like a storm is brewing in it. Suddenly, it clears. Marilyn gazes out, her eyes large. "Hello, everyone." Her voice is high and breathy. "I thought there'd be more fans here, on the anniversary of my death."

"There are loads more in the Blossom Ballroom, a bunch of them dressed like you," I say. "Would you like us to carry you upstairs?"

"Yes," she says. "Thank you."

"But first could you talk with my mother?" I ask.

The scent of coffee is strong by the mirror as my mother moves in close. She and Marilyn talk in such low tones that I can't hear what they're saying.

Other ghosts clamor for a turn at the mirror. After about ten minutes, Marilyn says to Junie and me, "Girls, it's time to meet my fans."

Junie carries one end of the mirror, while I grab hold of the other. We set it down in the ballroom, and the mirror is immediately swarmed by fans. Ms. Monroe smiles her big famous smile, her eyelids at half-mast.

chapter
thirty-seven

It's lunch, and our first meal back at home in Phoenix.

The Ruler cooked my favorite dish and invited Grandma over to celebrate our return and my *Hollywood Girl* award and how I broke up the Beverly Hills Bandits. Grandma's finally getting out and about a little since her hip surgery. She's moving slowly with a walker.

Sam pulls out her chair, and Grandma plunks down.

The Ruler sets a steaming glass pan on a hot pad in the middle of the table. I close my eyes and inhale. Überdelicious. Melted cheese with spinachy stuff, organic brown rice, and some unidentified junk thrown in there too. Cheesy chard.

I count silently in my mind, waiting for my dad to bust out his same lame-o pun. One, two—

"Cheesy chard, Paula?" Dad sticks his nose close to the casserole, like he's inspecting it. "I hope it's not overcooked. Or we'll have to rename it charred chard." He cracks up.

Sam cracks up too.

And even though The Ruler's heard this excuse-for-a-joke several times, her cheeks pink up and she smiles. She flits around the table, checking our water glasses and offering us bread. When she nears my dad, she clasps his shoulder. Like she can't quite believe he's home for real.

They grin big at each other. Watching my dad and The Ruler with their gaga eyes makes me realize I should add another line to my essay. True love can strike more than once in a lifetime. I hadn't really thought that far into the future when I wrote the essay.

"Sherry, could you grab the salad dressing?" The Ruler asks.

I meander over to the fridge and notice a balding bird with ratty wings perched outside on our kitchen sill. Grandpa! I quietly crack the window. The air-conditioning is on, and I'm not up for a lecture about energy and bills.

"Thanks," Grandpa croaks.

"No prob," I say quietly, then head back to the table with a bottle of ranch and a bottle of Italian.

"Let me get a close-up look at your necklace," Grandma says.

I slip it off and hand it to her.

"It's beautiful." Grandma holds the chain up high and the diamond dangles, catching the light. "You know, if you ever have any questions about true love, come to me. Your grandfather and I had a very special, long-lasting relationship."

Grandpa caws.

"Is that the bird from my backyard?" Grandma shakes her head in disbelief, and her short gray hair bounces. "Did he follow me all the way over here again?"

"It's definitely him," Sam says. "I'd recognize his sticky-out belly anywhere."

Poor Grandpa. I don't think Grandma is ever going to make the connection that he is who he is.

Suddenly I smell coffee.

"I'm out here with your grandfather," Mom says.

I raise my fork in a subtle hello.

"Sherry, I'm so very proud of you." The Ruler spears a lettuce leaf. "You win a contest with an essay, and you manage to solve a case that was baffling the police."

"It's like you're a magnet for mysteries," Sam says.

Sam's a brainiac like Junie. I keep waiting for him to figure out about the Academy of Spirits and Mom.

"Whatever happened to those girls?" Dad says.

"Their parents chose to leave them in juvenile hall. They'll be going to school there in the fall," Mom says. "David's in jail, waiting for a court date."

I repeat the info.

"How do you know all this?" Sam asks. That guy is too smart.

"I'm just sort of in the loop since I was a big part of the case." I sip some water, then excuse myself for a second.

I zip outside. "Mom, I'm dying to know. How did Real Time go with Dad?"

"It was nice," my mother says. "You know I can't really give you specifics. But we got some closure. And it was good to sit down with your father and chat about you and Sam."

Even knowing that small amount fills me with a warm glow like I just drank hot chocolate.

"Congratulations on wrapping up the Beverly Hills Bandits case," Grandpa says.

At least I'm pretty sure that's what he said. Sometimes all I hear from him is consonants.

"I'll bring Leah to see you later. She's excited about telling you what classes she'll be taking at the Academy." Mom gives me a light hug. "I wanted to stop by to make sure you got home okay."

After lunch, I tramp upstairs to my bedroom. The

glitz and glamour of Hollywood already seems distant and far away, like last Thanksgiving. Even Mark is a fading memory; I can only vaguely remember the sound of his voice.

I stand in my room, staring at my aquariums. Yes, I now have two. In tank #1, Cindy and Prince zip around in a joyous game of silvery tag. Below them, nestled in the gravel, are a bunch of tiny fish eggs. As soon as they hatch, I'll scoop them up with a net and move them over to the new tank. Because while Cindy and Prince are beautiful and fun to watch, they are not particularly good parents and would actually eat their babies.

Tank #2 is filled with water at seventy-seven degrees Fahrenheit and nicely decorated with plants and blue and pink gravel. And a partial rhinestone that was dug up many years ago from the cement in front of Grauman's Chinese Theatre.

Ms. Monroe gave the rhinestone piece to Mom after confessing that she tried to dig it up from her own stone for publicity. She also shared some of the details of her mysterious death with Mom, but swore her to secrecy! Why? Marilyn wants the mystery surrounding her death to remain. We aren't about to argue with her.

My cell pings with a text message.

<PLEASE meet me @ J.U. juice>

It's from Josh.
Before I have a chance to answer, another text pops up.

    <Ill order lrge strawberry
    swirl>

My favorite smoothie.

    <I have surprise for u>

Wow.

    <I wrapped it>

Double wow.
I type back. <Not J.U. juice> I want a clear brain when I see him. We have too many memories floating around the juice bar, and I'm afraid they'll latch onto me and cloud my thinking. Plus, he was just there with Olivia.

    <desserts r us?> Josh texts.

It's a tiny restaurant at the west end of the mall. Private. Delicious. Quiet background tunes.
Before I have a chance to reply, another text arrives. <so?>
And I type back one little letter.

I gaze at myself in the mirror hanging on the back of my bedroom door. Plaid shorts, a white tank under a peach shirt, matching peach lip gloss, dark eyes, a hint of mascara, wavy brown hair.

Do I need to change?

Do I need to redo my makeup?

Do I need to mess with my hair?

No, I'm fine just the way I am.

I let The Ruler know I'm going to the mall, and I step out into the hot, baking Arizona afternoon. Each flip-flopped step takes me closer to Josh. And closer to some kind of decision. I'm tingly all over, like I just scrubbed with citrus bath wash.

The mall's air-conditioning hits me with an arctic blast. As I approach Desserts R Us, I'm a weird mixture of nerves and calm. I can't even describe it.

Josh is already at a table. His skateboard is propped up in the corner. A rectangular box, wrapped in tissue, sits next to his elbow. He's looking at the menu. Josh glances up, like he senses my presence. Our eyes meet. He sets down the menu and stands. I move toward him. He opens his arms and I walk right into them.

Everything feels so right in that tight hug. From the familiar scent of chlorine mixed with laundry soap to the beat of Josh's heart.

Everything also feels so wrong. He did break up with me. He did choose polo over Hollywood. He did come to the mall and hold hands with another girl. A hug and a wrapped gift don't make all that disappear.

We both sit. The waitress arrives and pulls a pad and pencil from her apron pocket. I order mango cheesecake drizzled with tropical-fruit sauce. Josh orders a banana split.

He pushes the package across the table. "For you."

I unwrap it, slowly. From the shape, I know it's a video game. "Lifeline!" I've been wanting to get this game for a while. "Josh! It's so expensive! How did you ever afford it?"

"I traded some games in." He smiles, all proud, like he invented trade-ins.

I pull the Camel's Breath CD from my purse. "I got you something too."

"Where?" he sputters. "How?"

"Camel's Breath was the band at the awards dinner. They did an exclusive CD for *Hollywood Girl*."

He runs his fingers across the case. "Wow. Thanks."

Josh sets the CD down, then gazes at me with his blue, blue eyes. "I'm really sorry. Can we just get back together?"

"I don't think it's that easy. Stuff happened."

"About Olivia. I never wanted to go out with her. A varsity guy from the team set us up. I never met her before that day. We have nothing in common. I was thinking of you the whole time. She actually said,

'Gross,' when I suggested Video World. Then she took my hand. Then Brianna was there, and it all got messed up."

My elbows on the table, my chin is resting on the bridge formed by my hands. I don't say anything, just listen.

"And I am kind of freaked out that I'll be in high school, and you won't. But you're still the same person. Does it really matter where you go to school?"

Still listening.

The waitress arrives with our desserts. She glances first at me, then at Josh. She leaves. No doubt the air is charged with love and tension and indecision.

Josh digs into his ice cream. "You're right, Sherry. It's not that easy."

With the side of my fork, I carefully slice off a wedge of cheesecake. "Why don't we start with a video game? Lifeline. My living room. Saturday afternoon."

Josh's eyes sparkle like holiday lights. "Okay."

A fuzzy happy feeling, like a dandelion wish floating on a summer breeze, drifts up from my stomach and wafts past my heart. Whatever happens, I'll be fine. Even more than fine.

I raise the fork to my lips and my mouth fills with sweetness.

Barrie Summy grew up in Canada, about 2,500 miles away from Hollywood. She visited all the places in this book, bought loads of souvenirs, and discovered that she is not very good at recognizing famous people.

Now she lives in California with her husband, their four children, a poodle named Dorothy, two veiled chameleons, and an incubator full of chameleon eggs. Visit her at barriesummy.com.